Heggie Pump - Just Past the Blaze of Noon

A story by Sewel T. Whynot

To Elizabeth, James and Rebecca.

Published by Lewis Parnell Ltd
Copyright ©2014 Lewis Parnell Ltd

email: lewisparnell@btinternet.com

ISBN: 978-0-9576982-1-5

1

Prologue

Keith T. Armstrong and Hector (Heggie) Pump share a boundary in semi-rural Buckinghamshire, United Kingdom and the liking for a drink. Despite both being rich in life - for different reasons, something was itching at them. They were definitely scratching an itch, not itching a scratch.

They had reached a point in their lives where circumstances were fertile for an adventure. They had come to this point by very different trodden paths.

The events you are about to read are fictitious to say the least, designed to entertain and delight you. The 'accident', the shed gatherings, the caper in London, the venture, the bet and the big win at the bookies – made up. Heggie – made up. Heggie's family and acquaintances (the Police DI, the music man, the psychiatrist, the record scout and the eccentric 'The Hat') – sadly made up, as I'm sure you would like to bump into them all in real life. Relationships with the big groups such as Pink Floyd and Led Zeppelin and with Dennis Hopper and Jim Morrison would have probably happened. Keith – not entirely made up, based a bit on the author and his daily wrestles with his demons and life struggles; particularly in the pool. The baddies; the Robinson Brothers, the tattooed man and the American man, you will be pleased to note, don't exist - so you can sleep well.

Although the events and characters are fictitious, they are however, things that are happening around you, each and every day of the year. Take the time to look up – they are all there for you.....no excuses now.

Part 1

Heggie and Keith's Journey

Chapter 1

8th June 2013 (Keith's Birthday and the Day of the 'accident')

Keith felt veritably chipper for a man of 40 years as he snuggled in his bunk on board the Bahia Princess cruise liner. The cabin was warm and comfortable and the thick duvet folded and rippled around him in adequate proportions. The compactness of the cabin space gave him a sense of comfort; as if he was protected, wrapped up safely in the middle of the ship.

He lay there for a few minutes staring at the agreeable leaf patterned wallpaper on the wall. The semi-darkness of his cabin seemed to blur and spin and within seconds he whooshed out into the corridor. This wasn't an unpleasant experience in the slightest and it seemed inconsequential as his mother was there outside his door waiting for him.

Keith's cabin was at the very end of a run of doors and the corridor was long and narrow. They walked the corridor together admiring all of the interesting and colourful things to see. Keith's mum pointed out various curios as they went – Keith was always interested in what is mum had to say. The carpet was thick and plush, red with a lovely vivid bright yellow pattern on it. It was nice to walk on.

Keith glided effortlessly up the stairs and onto the communal walkway; almost as if he was being carried. He was on his own now as the corridor widened and became busier. The corridor was brightly lit by the blue sunshine reflecting off the sea and Keith could see the sea running to the unpunctured horizon through the large glass windows.

On his right were the usual booths, one to change money, one to seek assistance from the company staff as well as a number of small boutique shops selling expensive things that seem like a good idea to buy when one is on holiday.

On Keith's left, the bar had started and *'boy'*, Keith thought, *'what a bar!'* There was no access for Keith to the first part of the bar as it was behind large, heavy looking glass panels. Keith could only look in. Further along, however, Keith could simply walk from the hard flooring of the corridor onto the thin and efficient carpeted area just by stepping over the rather worn, but still shiny, gold strip.

'Lots of opportunities for a good drink,' thought Keith. He could see his two best chums at the bar and they gave him a wave. He could have a very nice chat with Neil and a good session on the fruit machines with Peter who was always feeding the fruties in order to 'get the win'. Either way, he could have a good, solid drink.

At the far end of the corridor, outside on the deck in the sunshine, Keith could see his wife and two children. They were silhouetted against the brightness of the sky which shone on their shoulders and around their heads. To his family was where he was heading.

As he approached the door that led out onto the deck, there was the same slight blurring and spinning as before, and uncontrollably, Keith was pulled through a doorway on his right - sucked almost. The large room was all iron with none of the softness of furnishings of the corridor. It was painted industrial grey which gave it a clean but clinically harsh feel. The starkness of the room

6

seemed to give Keith an acute pressure in the back of his head.

A small but immaculately turned out nurse in her white uniform was approaching Keith from the far end of the room. The room contained people, but Keith was fixed on the nurse. As he somehow expected, she was an older woman, with an air of seniority, and she certainly brought him some reassurance that this would be a well ordered area of the ship.

She seemed to take an age to reach him. Keith noticed in front of him, eight or so students all in climbing gear, huddled together and wearing their round orange and yellow peak-less helmets. They were loosely bound together by their climbing ropes and they leaned inwards together as a group. It appeared to Keith that they were set out as if they would be more suited to being on a mountain than in a cargo bay on a ship. There were other occupants, in ones and twos in the room, mainly standing quietly.

The quietness struck Keith. It was very quiet. One man was sat on the floor with a lady bending over him. Another man was standing looking at the wall as if he was staring into a mirror. It looked like he too had a headache as he held some painkillers. It was weirdly maddening but serene and everyone was quiet and calm. So quiet.

The nurse stood in front of Keith and introduced herself, but gave no name. Although she did not smile to any extent or show any real emotion, Keith felt comfortable in her presence.

There were two corridors running from the adjacent corners of the room. Keith noticed a man in a dark turtleneck jumper, dark trousers and a pair of tan moccasins creep into sight in the left hand corridor. Within a blink of an eye, the nurse shifted twenty of so meters and appeared in front of the corridor and blocked the man's entry into the room by standing in the opening.

Their exchange was quiet but Keith could hear the firm nature of the discussions. Keith felt they were discussing him, however the man was obscured by the gloom of the corridor and the position in which the nurse was standing so he couldn't get a sense of what they were talking about. The nurse politely ordered the man back down the corridor and he retreated partly; but not so far that he was unable to see Keith.

Keith watched the nurse walk directly to the other corridor. She was fast, efficient and controlled. Keith was sure that the corridor was directly facing south as the glare of the sun's reflection on the water filled it with bright sunlight, making it almost too bright to see anything. But Keith thought the sun was to his left – it was shining on the backs of his family who were to his left. Left was the way he was walking – this didn't make sense. Keith was disorientated and his head hurt like hell.

Keith could see the nurse consulting with someone but Keith couldn't quite see who due to the magnificent power of the brightness. She turned slightly and looked at Keith, turned back again to the corridor and nodded, as if having received instruction.

.oOo.

I am Keith's mind and we're not doing all that well at the moment. We have cranial swelling, skeletal damage to the ribs and left leg. For a while now I've been trying to repairs the heart, liver and kidneys, but that is not as a result of the 'accident'. I've shut everything down apart for the key functions whilst I try to sort this mess out. I'm allowing audio and smell only for Keith's wife, Katy and children Ford and Carina in the hope that this will aid healing. I've not done anything on this scale before. You might think I come with a manual or a built-in survival mode which kicks in at times like these, but no. So, I'm just doing what I'm doing and hoping. I'm also allowing audio access to Heggie Pump; as this will be good for Keith.

Chapter 2

18th July 1969

Detective Brookes took the incident sheet from his tray. He looked at it the same way he had looked at it the eight times previously - with sadness. Brookes was sad for himself and sad for this Heggie Pump.

Brookes rubbed his temples with the middle finger and thumb of his left hand and looked out of the window. 'I should be doing something else. The boy Pump should be doing something else. Enjoying the weather or something.'

Brookes again read the typing on the sheet in front of him.

'Heggie Pump – 16 years old. English National.

Resident with his biological mother, Thelma Pump, and her husband of 5 years, Frank Roberts. 116 Madison Boulevard, Edgartown, Martha's Vineyard, Massachusetts.

Heggie Pump missing since incident with Frank Roberts, 15th July 1969. Frank Roberts returned to the home after a long drinking session at Flo's Bar and Diner. Fight broke out between all three. Mr Roberts has submitted a charge against Heggie Pump of attempted homicide. Mrs Pump states it should be the reverse and has lodged a complaint against her partner, Mr Roberts.'

'Great,' Brookes sighed. 'The boy Pump could be anywhere in the US, or even back in England by now.' He paused and considered the situation again. 'Leave it. That nasty piece of work Roberts will probably sober up and drop charges.'

Brookes looked out of the precinct window and across the park with its hazy sunshine and the college kids and families enjoying their summer vacation break. He looked at the picture on his desk of his kids, all grown up now. He paused and considered the situation a further time. It was eating at him. He considered what made him just want to leave it in the hope that it would all resolve itself. Two more months until retirement and his wish of endless fishing trips. He was looking forward to the autumn in his boat. He wished to be free and do his own thing. He'd wished his life away. His children looked out at him from the desk.

'This just ain't right. I'm gonna put that drunk freak Roberts inside. It's about time he stayed away from the public for a while. The boy Pump is probably innocent and should be concentrating on perfecting his loops at the skate park and not hiding out from the Police. Do the right thing Brookes,' he told himself.

Chapter 3

19th July 1969

Heggie Pump walked up to the festival entrance.

It was risky. The Police may be looking for him here. He couldn't be sure as he had been out of circulation for a couple of days; laying low with friends. It was a calculated gamble to try and see his mum. She would be there – she wouldn't miss The Boston Stranglers playing right on her doorstep and she knew Heggie would try and make contact with her sometime - and this would be a likely place as any.

Heggie put his money on most of the local Police being back at the precinct watching the Apollo 11 lunar landing or down at Poncha Pond investigating the death of Mary Jo Kopechne and just why Senator Ted Kennedy hadn't reported driving his car off the bridge for over 10 hours.

No trouble at the gate as he handed over his entrance dollars. He made his way to the side right as far forward towards the stage as he could go. He looked back on the illuminated, trance like porcelain faces. With 40,000 fans looking towards the stage and one person looking back at the crowd, he knew people would think he was a weirdo and he would certainly raise suspicion amongst the security. After about half an hour of casually glancing back at the crowd and systematically studying batches of faces, he spotted her.

The warm evening air carried the music well and his closeness to the speakers vibrated his chest and lifted him into the beats of the drums. He made his way to her, even the recent events couldn't keep her from missing this. Man, he felt bad. Desolate. Everything had been ruined.

He was next to her now, both gazing forward to the band.

'I don't know how they manage to be so good live,' he shouted.

She didn't move her eyes from stage; that would draw attention to him.

'Son,' she said, 'it's not your fault. I've made a terrible mistake taking up with Frank. It's too dangerous for you to come back right now. He's demanding you're arrested and tried for attempted homicide. You know the law, it don't protect the innocent in these cases.'

She continued swaying to the music of the band but then she stopped, turned to him and said, 'I'm gonna mount a campaign to petition that jurisdiction - but in the meantime, you've got to hide yourself away. Here's some money, I thought you might try and find me here. Jesus will protect you Heggie, take all the help he offers you. Go now; I'm sure they will be trailing me.'

They hugged each other tightly as only a mother and son could and she kissed him several times on his face.

Heggie made his way from the festival, back through the crowds and out past the gate security. He walked through the dusty row of cars, baked by the day's sun and covered with a fine dust film. He was headed for the nearest highway.

A door of a sports car swung open and blocked his way between vehicles. Heggie stopped dead in his tracks, his heart thumped and his stomach rolled right over. The car park wasn't lit so Heggie couldn't see who was in the car. Not a police car. Surely the FBI aren't on this – no, that would be stupid. *'Frank,'* he thought to himself.

A tall fella emerged from the car, tight t-shirt, blue jeans and pumps. *'Not Frank.'* The man looked like he was slow and confused. Heggie figured that he had probably taken some low grade acid or something.

A woman started shouting at him from in the car. *'Definitely not the Police.'*

'Aw come on Diane,' the tall fella said. 'I couldn't care less if this is the car that me and Mable first got together in – shit, it's a car, that's all, a hundred dollar car. It gets me from the flat to the mall and around town.' He slammed the door and raised his hands to the stars and stumbled around slightly. The berating from the woman appeared to have livened him up a little.

The woman threw a lipstick at the windshield and shrieked some more. Heggie so didn't want the attention. The security guards would be taking a closer look if this went on, maybe even the Police.

'That's her lipstick, Earl. Change the car - you would if you loved me.'

Diane clambered out from the passenger side. She was skinny, pale and white with big hair combed back and lots of bangles. She pushed her sleeves up over her thin forearms as far as her elbows. Life hadn't been kind to her. Earl knew he was heading for trouble. Heggie knew he needed to beat a retreat.

'Hey buddy!' Earl cried out, now noticing Heggie and thinking that he might just save him from more of an onslaught from Diane. 'You drive?'

'I'm learning.' Heggie answered.

'Hell, it don't matter anyway, take the car,' Earl said, tossing Heggie the keys and circling his hand high around in the air and finally rested it in a point at Heggie and bounced, 'my present to you.'

14

Earl swung round and faced Diane. 'Issue over honey – and I'm getting me a beer, seeing as I ain't driving again this evening.'

Heggie lowered himself into the driver's seat. *'Full tank of gas, two nearly-full packs of Marlboros and even a baseball cap and sunglasses in case I need them,'* he said to himself. *'Where to then Heggie?'* he asked himself. After a moment's pause, *'West Coast,'* he answered.

He slid the key into the ignition and the old car started. 'Accelerator, brake, clutch down, into gear, wait for the bite'. He pulled slowly out of the car park and headed for the sea.

Chapter 4

23rd July 1969

Heggie looked out over the ocean from Santa Monica Boulevard. The southern Californian sun baked his face and the sea air filled his lungs. It felt good. The noise from the sea, the wind and the pleasure-makers on the beach seemed to carry away his worries. He turned his face into the full sun, closed his eyes and feasted on his ham baguette. The world must be okay if he was having a ham baguette, white bread with a little bit too much butter.

He fingered the LA Times music supplement and re-read the review of the Edgartown festival.

'.....and whilst The Boston Stranglers prepared for their encore, the crowd were entertained by local campaigner, Thelma Pump, who gave a rallying and entertaining, if not out-of-place speech on how she was going to change the law on self defence within murder charges. "For too long, the good folk of America have been wrongly imprisoned for just defending themselves from lunatics and alcoholics". 'Amen,' the band replied and dedicated their finishing number, "I just gotta shake you off - you old drunk" to Mrs Pump'.

Heggie flipped over the picture postcard of Santa Monica Bay, complete with dolphins and palm trees, took another bite of his baguette and wrote:

'Dear Thelma. Heard about the campaign and if I wasn't looking for work right now, I'd be

campaigning with you. I wish you every success and am right behind you.'

He filled in the address, placed the stamp on the allotted space upside down, just like he had always done when he was away from home and writing back to his mum, and mailed it.

Back behind him, outside the arena on Carolina Street, two artic lorries pulled up. The local Police laid out the traffic cones, got back into their squad cars and drove away.

A group of 10 or so men of assorted appearance, different facial and skin apparel, probably with questionable backgrounds Heggie thought, alighted and were directed into the backstage area by the arena security.

Heggie watched the big biceps in black t-shirts pushing big black boxes with big black boots. *'They must do this in every arena across the state. Easy access to the whole of the USA probably. Useful,'* Heggie thought, *'easy to travel, unnoticed.'*

'You looking for work buddy?' the roadie in charge shouted across in the direction of Heggie, 'pay you by the hour – we're short and gotta get rigged by four.'

Heggie opened his mouth to answer.

'I'm afraid I'm rather too busy, 'came a haughty but friendly voice from behind Heggie.

Heggie turned and looked over his shoulder. The chief roadie craned his neck so he could see past Heggie to the person who'd replied. The voice had come from a vagrant who was sat crossed legged on the bench, reading Heggie's music supplement and making himself up a baguette from Heggie's ham and bread. The vagrant looked up and away to buy him some more time whilst he assembled his find.

17

'Why not?' Heggie replied to the roadie in charge, 'I'm free at the moment.'

'Any experience?'

'No, but I got a black t-shirt.'

'Well, that will have to do.'

Heggie turned to the bum. 'Hey buddy, you drive?'

'It's been a while.'

'Then take the keys to this car, a gift from the good Lord.'

'That ain't no car,' the bum said, rubbing his hands together and making out the curves of the sports car in the air – that's a fine motel!'

Chapter 5

13th August 1969

The Highway sign read 'Atlanta City Limits'.

'Right people, prepare to disembark in 15 minutes, wake-up and sober up fast if you need to,' said big fat Geoff.

Big fat Geoff was the lead roadie who had hired Heggie some three months earlier. The others only called him that when he wasn't listening otherwise he was sure as hell would crush their heads if he heard them. He stood at least 6½ foot high and impressively, was just as wide.

'Atlanta arena, last leg of the US Tour,' Geoff announced to the troupe as he strode down the bus. He stopped where Heggie was laid on his makeshift bunk between the spare cables and a dozen high stack of beer slabs.

'Heggie, you're paid up in full and you've paid all your dues so you're free to go after we pack up tonight. I don't know where's you headin' or what you're running from, but you're welcome to stick with us if you want. The next stop is a festival gig at a place called Woodstock. They say it's not going to be that big a festival, a 'music and art Festival' they're calling it by all accounts, but it should be fun.'

Heggie looked out of the bus window at the lights passing on the freeway. He could see the suburban houses of Atlanta. Perhaps he would stay on until Woodstock – that sounded a little bit villagey, like his homeland, England. He had seen too much of the gizzards of metropoli. Heggie asked himself what was to become of him. He wasn't sure where he was going and if he was really running. He needed some direction.

A wave of optimism flushed over him. It did that sometimes. He was a positive guy. He opened up the letter he has just written and read it again.

'Dear Themla. I've been travelling so much that I haven't had the chance to write. I can't believe that the campaign is going so well, so quickly. I read in the nationals that the Senate are going to debate the issue. I'm so damn proud of you. Although I can't help by being with you, hopefully the enclosed postal check will go some way to covering your campaign expenses. With Frank in gaol, I expect it is tough to make ends meet.'

Heggie folded the cheque into the letter, neatly placed it in the envelope, did the stamp thing and the next day he mailed it from the small town of Woodstock.

Chapter 6

18th August 1969

Heggie was on the stage finishing packing up the set for the Boston Stranglers. He felt it was time to get off the tour.

'Would you tune the instruments for my band? We're on next,' a thin man asked him. 'You see I'm dressed in velvet and I couldn't possibly do it myself!'

Heggie checked him out. He was indeed dressed head to toe in velvet. 'No,' Heggie was just about to answer.

'Velvet, velvet!' the thin man shrieked. 'How louche am I?' he asked his hanger on-ers. 'Kings, Cardinals and me! Stroke it, go on,' he continued to his adoring snouts. 'Dark and naughty isn't it,' he said at Heggie, 'the jacket is hammered and the cloak is crushed!'

Freaked by this oddball, who looked like a cross between a vampire and a chair in an old peoples' home, Heggie leapt up onto the adjoining stage where the thin man's instruments were. He had no idea just who the thin man was, but there were about 120 thousand people in the audience waiting for him.

'We want Woodpecker,' they were chanting.

Heggie's presence on stage roused them further and they chanted even louder. They were now expecting the performance to be imminent. Heggie tuned up the drums best he could; he wasn't sure if drums needed tuning or not. He plucked a few of the strings on the lead guitar as he didn't know any chords and made out he was pretty important. His roadie career before had always been backstage, linking cables, pushing boxes and drinking beer afterwards.

The band came on and the crowd erupted.

Heggie handed the guitar to an equally thin man who gave him a polite and very English 'thank-you'. The lead guitarist was quite dissimilar to the velvet clad singer, but then they usually are different. He wore a nicely considered, ultra slim timepiece by Vacheron Constantin and an immaculately cut dove grey suit which was elegantly ahead of its time. The Englishman encouraged Heggie to stay on the stage by offering him some supporting instruments. Heggie stayed and played the tambourine on the first song and the canastas on the second. 'I could be involved in all this music biz,' Heggie sang out loud as he shook his canastas for all he was worth.

Chapter 7

Man in the Shed. 8th April 2013

'There's someone in the shed, Dad,' whispered Carina, cupping her hands around her mouth to give the situation some excitement but seeming not in the slightest bit concerned that there was a stranger on her territory.

'Is there?' Keith responded.

'He looks like a buffoon,' she continued with the spring sun glinting in her eyes and shining through her blonde hair.

'Let's have a look shall we princess,' replied Keith.

They went to the patio doors together and stood side by side, hands on hips; Daddy and his supergirl.

'Ah, that's Hector Pump, Heggie to his friends. He lives at the end of our garden.'

'He actually lives at the end of our garden? That can't be right Dad, can it?' Well, she was only five years old so anything seemed possible to her, but she was used to her Dad's tall tales.

'No, I meant he lives in the big old house that backs onto our garden. I haven't quite worked it out yet - but he has taken to using our shed as a music listening studio. He comes through a magical portal in the hedge to use our shed. Poor chap; I don't think he has a shed of his own. What you can't see is the person laid down in Auntie Hazel's chair, probably someone rich and famous.'

'Have you seen anyone rich and famous Dad in our shed?' chipped in Ford who joined them at the patio door and now alert to the possibility of meeting a 'face'. 'Any footballers?' Well, he was eight, football was all he thought of really.

Keith paused and thought for a moment. 'Well no, they've always seemed to have been some poor soul who just happens to cross paths with Heggie, or they are his old and dear friends - as eccentric as he is.'

Keith sat on the sofa and gathered his children around him by patting a space on each side of him. 'I met Heggie about a month ago, it was during that unfeasibly sunny spell in February. I think Heggie must be one of those people who hibernate all winter and he had just woken up.'

'Really Dad?' Carina asked scrunching her nose up. 'Do I hibernate?'

'Only bears hibernate Carina,' said Ford, quite matter of fact. 'Mr Tang taught us that at school.'

'Yes, kiddies don't hibernate - they might miss Christmas and that wouldn't be much fun would it now.'

Carina didn't quite know where she was with this now and she stood up again pondering and looking back towards the shed, an arm on one hip, slightly bent in the middle of her body and twisting around on her pointed toes.

'The gloom of winter,' Keith continued, 'had just lifted from the garden in early February and the weather was making a promising start to the year. You know this always raises my expectations of a fantastic summer! The early-year sunshine is like a shot in the arm for me and I try to grab what time I can in the garden. Let me tell you kids, the reason Heggie pump is in our shed is all Queen's fault.'

'What, THE Queen?' asked Carina.

'No the rock group Queen. You know...*another one bites the dust...and another one gone and another one down, hey I'm gonna get you too...another one bites the dust...hey hey hey hey hey hey hey heeey.*'

24

Keith didn't even like Queen, he thought they were a bit sad. Now The Doors, or a bit of Floyd or even a bit of the Manic Street Preachers was where it was at. Queen were Keith's brother's favourite band. Keith had sold all his brothers Queen records at a car boot when he was 17 years old for a quid each, he had that much regard for them.

One Saturday afternoon however, Keith's opinion had been challenged. Ford and Carina had linked Ford's iPod to their plastic fantastic karaoke machine, and yes, Queen had been belted out. After hearing hook-lines from various luke warm early Saturday evening game shows, Ford had downloaded the greatest hits of Queen. Hit after hit was warbled out, all through the album. Keith remembered them all and enjoyed each of them. He did silly dances and sung along, just for the children's sake you understand.

That afternoon had got him thinking about music, he used to love his music – what happened here? He never listened to music anymore. What happened to the Specials, Madness, Lynyrd Skynyrd? Keith spent most of his early teen years listening to music on his Sony walkman. 'I'm just off to revise,' he would tell his parents when he was doing his 'O' Levels and would be found two hours later asleep still listening to his walkman. The only thing that curtailed his music listening in those days was the cost of batteries to run the walkman.

That evening, after a few glasses of red wine, Keith even lightened up about Queen. Ford had loaded some of Keith's albums onto his iPod Keith had bought him for his birthday; he was pleased that Ford seemed to be setting out on his very own musical journey. What pleased Keith even more was that his bank of CDs, which hadn't been touched for so long, so long in fact that Keith didn't even see them any more in the bookcase, were being enjoyed again.

In bed that night, Keith listened to all the ecliptic tracks Ford had downloaded onto his iPod. Keith found again how sensational it was to submerge himself in the bubbling melodies and hard southern guitar riffs of Lynyrd Skynyrd's 'Pronounced' album and the gritty electric sounds of The Specials.

There was a connection to what he was listening to, the familiarity, the memories, the intricacies of the ensemble, the respect he had for the artists and of course the basic feeling of pleasure. It was a weird but nice sensation to be cocooned with the music from the earphones being so firmly inserted into his ears, but yet he was worried that the beat of the music and the light from the screen of the iPod might disturb his delightful and well turned out wife.

A pillow over the head – that would do it. Keith didn't like the idea of not being able to hear the kiddies cry out or should his wife say something, so every now and again, he took one ear-piece out - just to check.

In the morning, Keith woke to find himself half strangled by the earphone wire and an excruciating pain in his ear from sleeping all night with the mini-speaker still in. The player had run through endlessly all night and the battery was flat. Ford had woken and came flying out through his bedroom door like a cannonball. Of course he spotted his iPod and wanted to listen to some music. Kids these days seemed to take to technology so very well and were comfortable with being isolated from the real world, just going about their business, Keith thought. For someone like Keith though, it was new and his generation were migrants to it. To Ford's generation it was just the norm.

Ford wasn't upset about his battery being flat; he was rarely upset with technological issues or with whatever his Dad did. Keith couldn't help feeling that he had been involved in something illicit the night before.

Circumstance was playing with Keith on his way to work the next morning. The paperboy nearly knocked him off his bike because he was listening to his music through his earphones and didn't hear Keith coming. It was dark, but Keith was sure the milkman had a pair of earphones in. The overweight grungy looking fella - walking very slowly, as usual, to the station was at it. Most of the people in Keith's train carriage were doing it and the underground was full of them. Keith made his way to his new office and even there, some of the cool young guys sat at their desks with headphones on.

Keith was a jobbing contractor. Some called him a 'consultant', some a 'project manager'; at the start of a new contract, Keith called himself 'miserable'. It was all new again and for the first few weeks of any contract he told himself over and over again that things would get better. They always did, but Keith felt this was no way to live. There has to be a better way Keith would tell himself - usually as he walked across the concourse and out of Marylebone station towards Baker Street tube station.

'I'd like my own business,' he would declare to himself, *'a sandwich bar – that would be great, enough to live on and a bit for savings and shut up shop early afternoon - perfect. A gardener perhaps – yes, that would do, a free man, working with nature, dirt under the fingernails and all that. Apart from the cold it would be just right. Better*

27

still, I could make a fortune on the horses if I studied hard enough. Mmm, not great at picking winners up till now though.'

Keith's recent contracts had been in London so he had the added pain of the daily commute. Not only did this extend Keith's day and more time away from his family, it gave him time to think – too much time to think and drink. On the positive side, he had fun people watching.

Chapter 8

'Duende'

Keith met some interesting people in his work. He always got on well with people. He was good at what he did, suffered with bouts of self doubt, but always managed to find the common ground with everyone in some way. Keith provided business support and assistance with planning improvements to organisations.

Everyone was interesting and that was saving Keith. One of the most interesting and complex character he met was a 'proper' consultant called Martin. Martin was a big hitter in the improvement world, respected, serious, sometimes a tad dour and a man of few words. When he spoke, people listened and the words just seemed like gold. Keith liked Martin's confidence and how comfortable Martin appeared with himself.

Keith and Martin's paths crossed a couple of times in different roles and at different locations and they kept in contact. It was always good to get a reality check every now and then and for Keith to know he wasn't the only one who had a hard time in convincing people 'change was good'.

Keith met up with Martin and another jobbing contractor, Sasinda in London one night. Sasinda, you could say, was the complete opposite of Keith – height, width, gender, background, religion and heritage. Keith had interviewed her for a post and he distinctly remembered feeling he wouldn't get on well with her, but he knew she'd be able to do the job. They were still chums a good few years later and Keith trusted her which, you certainly needed in Keith and Sasinda's game.

At dinner that evening, Martin unfolded a fascinating insight into his feelings and the man he was. His bright, penetrating eyes transfixed Keith and his words transported Keith to Sanlucar, 'the real Spain'.

'I bought this most wonderful villa in Sanlucar, Andalucia,' Martin said. 'Sanlucar sits on the left bank of the Guadalquivir river. My pension was doing nothing, so I bought it as the main part of my future plans. It's beautiful and overlooks the bay. It is a million miles away from the whitened teeth and enhanced cleavages of the British ex-pat enclaves.'

Martin talked about music, widely at first, about the concerts he had been to and his favourite artists. He had bought a very large screen TV and put it in the smallest room in his house so he could watch concerts. Leonard Cohen, highly acclaimed writer, poet, songman and Companion of the Order of Canada (the highest civilian award Martin advised) seemed to be his favourite and he told Keith and Sasinda about Leonard's 'Songs of Leonard Cohen' album. Keith was impressed, not only with Leonard but also the dedication to the artist - this was some years before home cinemas became fashionable.

Martin asked Keith's opinion on music and asked him if he had heard of a few artists. Keith felt his shortcomings in the music world surfacing, he wasn't going to lie but he knew Martin wasn't trying to find him out either.

'Two songs will sum it up,' Keith declared, 'Elton John's 'Tiny Dancer' always makes the hairs on the back of my neck stand up. It doesn't matter how many times I hear it or if I hear it twenty times in succession, I just don't tire of it. The second has it all. The passion, the excitement, the romance and the sexual electricity. Can you guess what it is?'

Sasinda and Martin were racking their brains and made a few guesses. 'How could a song have those many qualities in it? It must be the greatest song of all time,' they suggested to Keith, 'but why can't we guess it!'

'Cococabanna by Barry Manilow!' Keith announced. *'music and fashion were always the passion at the .... Coco ... bom, bom, bom .... they fell in love!'* he sang.

They had to agree, even out of part politeness.

It was a very personal choice this music stuff.

'Sanlucar,' Martin continued 'is famous for the Manzanilla, a variety of fino sherry and for the prawns; which are just wonderful. It is also internationally recognised for beach horse racing, which you would love Keith and for flamenco.' Keith raised his glass of wine in appreciation of the horse racing acknowledgement.

'Sanlucar sits opposite Donana, the national park and within that national park lies the 'Marisma de Hinojos' – literal translation is the salt marsh of fennel plants, some believe it to be the lost city of Atlantis. My favourite time is the 'noches de Bajo de Guia' which means the 'nights of the area by the sea' and it starts the festival of flamenco. I adore the flamenco!'

'Flamenco! Flamenco and Leonard Cohen? It's an unusual mix I'll give you that,' said Keith, 'but then so is, I suppose, Elton John and Barry Manilow!'

'Duende.' Martin spoke this word in passionate but hushed tones and provided even more drama by raising his hand with his fingers outstretched. Keith had never heard this word before.

'Duende,' Martin mouthed, even quieter as if he was addressing a taboo or revealing an underground secret, 'is about connecting as closely as possible to the music and the artist. He painted a vivid picture of the bar near his villa where he often listened to flamenco music being performed. These were Martin's warm feelings and memories and Keith could feel the vibe. Martin described the scene in detail. He had that far away misty and dreamy look in his eyes and was quite different from the direct way he operated in the work environment.

Keith could picture the tables and chairs where Martin was sat. They were dark wood and contrasted vividly with the lighter colours of an old brick and render pillar. The pillar formed part of an alcove and provided a bit of privacy but gave Martin an unobstructed view of the artist.

Keith could smell the wine and the tapas mingling in the air, powerful, spicy and pungent smells. It was early evening, the sky outside was still bright. The bar however was dark; the sun knew not to disturb the atmosphere in there. Keith could picture Martin, sat only a few feet away from the artist, absorbed into the music and the performance and mesmerised by the swirling of the bright red dress and heavy thud of the dancer's shoes on the well worn wooden floor. The floor would have witnessed many an age of dancer, generations of local women winning their passage of rite to perform there - with the sum of the music and dancer creating something much more than the two separate parts.

Keith was pleased for Martin that he seemed to have found something so pleasurable and he enjoyed thinking of it himself.

The conversation throughout the evening was lively and interesting. Sasinda made many a great reveal of startling incidents and things that has happened to her in her life.

'I lived for a while in a basement that was used by the couple who owned the house as a bondage den. The rent was cheap but I had to make myself scarce when they wanted to use the room. Another time I was held for 24 hours at the Saudi/Qatar border. Somehow the Saudi Royal family found out which family I was from and I was invited to afternoon tea at the Tuwaiq Palace. Rather a different situation to smoking rollups with the guards on border control. I didn't see Battenberg cake until I was six and went to a party for the first time. I just love it when you buy me 'window' cake Keith!'

Much ground was covered as well as a good quantity of robust red wine. By comparison to the other's, Keith's life had followed a fairly traditional path but Keith knew he was richly blessed with his life and his family. He felt though, that he could have had some of the excitement of Sasinda's escapades or found a truly amazing place to listen to music as Martin had. Keith's Inter-railing around Europe was pretty cool, but somehow not quite on the same scale.

Keith made his way home, it was late and he wobbled his way up the hill from Great Missenden train station on his bike. The darkness was consuming.

The pathway is narrow and runs alongside the wood which sweeps downwards and then away left into the valley. The wood seems to have its own consciousness and collective knowledge built up over centuries. These woods had seen generations coming and going. The woods appeared to be breathing all around Keith. Far from being unnerving, it gave Keith comfort.

These were the woods where Enid Blyton had walked and written her adventures of the Famous Five and Roald Dahl had taken his grandchildren

33

and told them scary stories of highwaymen and giants, of goblins and nasty grown-ups who always got their just deserts. These woods and the surrounding fields were the scenes of some of Dahl's most interesting work about local people, their incredible characteristics and outrageous escapades.

Great Missenden is littered with the landmarks referred to in Dahl's books. The garage and pumps from 'Danny Champion of the World', Sophie's Cottage which she called 'norphanage' in 'The Big Friendly Giant and the sweet shop from the Pelly, the Giraffe and me. Keith was immensely proud of this Dahl heritage and had visited his grave a few times up at St Peter and St Paul's church when Ford and Carina had harvest festivals and Christmas carol concerts there.

Keith loved the footprints of the Big Friendly Giant which led to his grave from the bench in the cemetery. Keith had attended a meeting at the school about the importance of reading with and to his children. Keith didn't read books, none in fact since he was about 16 years old. Mrs Thompson, the school headmistress had done the introduction. 'We are in Dahl territory! When Matilda realised that the local library contained books of wonderful stories she knew she would never be alone again. It gives me goose bumps every time I read that passage. Matilda was talking about our library, the one at the end of Great Missenden High Street!'

Keith was slow up the hill, his bike was slow – a racer, a gift from his brother in law. Keith liked to think the bike was a bit retro now being 20 years old but it was just a bit decrepit with a gearing mechanism that seemed to work against him and slip into gear number two as he reached the steepest part of the hill.

Keith had a brain which ensured he had an untroubled journey through life. Never taking on the bad things and excluding the overly intellectual thoughts. Although Keith had heard some fascinating tales earlier that evening, 'duende' had stuck in his uncomplicated mind.

It stuck and excited Keith for days. Keith had found a connection with Queen and although he told himself it was only a small one, he couldn't deny it. Keith experimented with getting that connection again. Sometimes he experimented late at night and sometimes after a glass of red wine. Keith dropped Ford at a party at High Wycombe leisure centre and even spent the intervening time in the John Lewis sound studio. He had once seen a film where an art collector sat in a darkened room and concentrated solely on one illuminated picture, sweating profusely and getting over excited.

He imagined he was Martin. Although the sofa in John Lewis was very comfortable and the music system was second to none, it was a bit difficult to concentrate with the Saturday salesperson waxing lyrically about differences between the Wharfedale 360 speakers and the 420 speakers. Keith had re-joined his musical journey.

Chapter 9

In Pursuit of the Ultimate 400 Meters Freestyle, Part 1 (The Re-start)

There were three specific of conversations which triggered Keith re-start of his swimming career. Swimmers called their time in the pool 'careers' which is an unusual concept given that you don't earn any money from it. It might be stretching a point, but you have to work at it and you do progress up the ladder in terms of status and performance.

Conversation 1

'Happy Anniversary darling wife!' Keith handed over his card and a gift bag. There was already a bottle of his favourite wine and a card waiting on his bedside cabinet for when he woke.

Katy opened her present.

'That's very thoughtful, thank you.'

'Thirteen wonderful years I've given you,' Keith said cheekily. The card Keith had chosen read 'Happy anniversary to my wife. You are the best! And I am the luckiest', and he was. 'Thirteen years is a long time but it's gone so quick,' Keith continued. 'I don't think we are any different, do you?'

'I feel the same but we'll both be 40 this year, it is time to start looking after ourselves. I'm worried we're drinking too much.'

'If only she knew how much,' Keith thought to himself.

'And if I could just tone up, that would be good.'

'I've put on a few pounds again,' Keith sighed.

'Around the chin in your case.'

'Which chin,' Keith asked cheerily, but he knew too well that he was a bit of a wobbler in this area, not too much, but enough for it to bulge when he lowered his head.

'It doesn't suit you. It will all be setting as we get older. Now is our chance to sort it out.'

That lunchtime, Keith bought himself a pair of Tempo Senior silver and green running shoes at the value sports shop. On the way home he even forwent his slim line gin and tonic cans from Sainsbury's and agreed that it was time to hit the pool.

Conversation 2

Keith arranged to meet his old swim buddy, Ben at Amersham pool for a dip before work. Nothing too strenuous as they agreed by text, just a gentle 'loosener' of the shoulders.

Ben and Keith swam together as juniors, following each other up and down the pool for what seemed like an endless amount of years. They knew each other pretty well and had shared rooms when they had gone to major events such as the Nationals.

Their friendship had lasted well beyond their training and competition days and they had followed similar paths with giving up swimming, putting on weight, getting really unfit, getting married, having children and pursuing a proper career which paid them a salary.

Keith packed his trunks and goggles, cycled to the station in the pitch dark, for it was very early, caught the train, alighted at Amersham and walked to the pool. He met Ben and they shook hands – it had been a while since they had seen each other.

Both were large with a fairly hefty middle spread and they went into the pool for warm up.

'Wow, that feels creaky!' said Ben after 400 meters mix swimming.

'My shoulders are hurting already!' agreed Keith.

'Let's do a set of 75's on different strokes with some decent rest.'

'Agreed, but I'm not doing any fly for now – I need to build up slowly.'

It was tough for the both of them. In the past it would have been easy. Swimming moulds the muscles into the correct form given that it is an unusual action with so much water resistance. They both felt really out of shape.

'Give it a couple of weeks and I'm sure we're going to start to feel the benefit and get some power back,' Ben said reassuringly; although he was still panting a fair bit as they took a shower. 'Did you see the results from the National Master's meet?'

'Not been following any swimming really,' Keith replied, helping himself to Ben's shampoo.

'You remember Andy who I shared a house with in Coventry when I was at college? He won the 400 front crawl at the National Masters last week and reckons that he might have a sniff of the British Master's record within the year.'

'What kind of distance is he doing then?'

'Swims six times a week, fit as a fiddle and winning medals again.'

'That's a big commitment.'

'You used to beat him all the time if I remember correctly.'

Conversation 3

38

'I swam this week,' Keith said to super fit, international amateur tri-athlete Alan.   They were both watching their children swimming up and down in the pool below at the club session. Their children had started in stoke improvers together and were doing very well now that they had made it into the big pool and 'Transition 1'.

'How did it go?' Alan asked.

'I swam like a baboon with cramp. Do you know what that looks like?'

'Can't say I do, no.'

'It's not nice to see Alan.   All pretty lamentable.'

'I had some coaching this week on my swimming. It's okay for you having had the years of swimming but for me, the swimming is not as natural. I went to see a chap in Reading, says he knows you from your swimming days.'

'I should have done something like coaching, or physiotherapy.   Something around sport. Unreasonable hours though. How is the training going?'

'It's going well thanks.   Building up for the World Triathlon Championships in Israel in April.'

'Ah, the 'Team GB' one.'

'I've joined the Masters group here to give me some discipline.   They've got some great swimmers; you'll fit in well and could probably lead the lane.'

They were joined on the balcony by Steve. Like three characters from the Muppets, they sat watching their children doing tumble turn practice and feeling each and every bumped foot on the side.

'I sold my bike this week,' Steve said.

'That's an unusual declaration Steve!' Alan said, surprised.

'I thought I should stop chasing my youth. I'm nearer 50 than 40 now and the back keeps going.'

'Ahh, man,' said Keith. 'I'm just starting to think about chasing my youth again. This is a blow Steve – you swim in lakes and things, you just can't go selling your bike. It's symbolically bigger than just the sale of a bit of kit.'

'There comes a time, you'll understand in due course.'

Steve's statement of fact terrified Keith.

There they sat. The 'wannabe again' just starting out on another fitness campaign, the 'contented ex-wannabe' with no bike and the 'doing it still and doing it to a very high level'.

Keith let his tummy slouch out a bit in disappointed acceptance.

'You know what you need Keith?' asked optimistic Alan.

'A bike?' Keith replied. 'I'm too late, Steve's already sold it.'

'No, a target. Something to train for. How about a 400 meters frontcrawl in a masters' event later in the year. You won't make 1500 meters these days as you are a bit too clapped out. 200 meters is probably a bit sharp for you and you'll get mullered by the fit guys so it will have to be the 400 meters; one of your old events.'

'Mmm, that's a bit of pressure. I'm not sure I have the time really to train properly.'

'You're wimping out already.'

'I would truly love to get in there. I'll have to think about it.'

'I bet you've got your trunks on now haven't you, under your trousers.'

'How did you know that?'

'It's just the way you're sat!'

'Seeing Ford swimming in the club brings it all back. The smell of the chlorine, the whiff of fitness around the sports centre, the sun coming through those windows and falling on the ripples of the water. I loved swimming here in the mornings. Starting off in the dark of a morning and then seeing the sun hit the water for the first time that day.'

'Make time, swim during your lunch hours. There must be pools near to where you are working. The Club Champs are coming up, I'll see if they do a Dad's race.'

'I'll have to have a think. I don't want to be heat 1, lane 1 again and a 50 meters dash is not really my event.'

Secretly though, Keith could feel the butterflies in his stomach; and it felt good.

Keith left the other two to it, talking about bikes and swimming in lakes with weed getting tangled around your legs. Keith surreptitiously checked the swimming club notice board for the race results for the masters. There were some very respectable times, but Keith thought he might be able to match some of them. He took comfort that a couple of his old records were still standing. And so too were Ben's – those were the glory years.

Chapter 10

Heggie Pump

The next day, the rest of the family were out visiting so Keith had some time to himself. Keith's garden was large and surrounded on all sides by well established trees and hedges.

At the bottom of the garden on the far right was a shed, a large shed with windows on the front facing the house. It was underutilised and Keith hadn't properly kitted it out since they had bought the house some 10 years previously. The garden wasn't overlooked because of the trees and the house at the back was set a long way back. Keith borrowed Ford's music station. He locked the side gate and went into the shed, set up Auntie Hazel's reclining garden chair - one of a set of two she had given them when she went to live in Spain.

Keith slid Marillion's 'Misplace Childhood' album into the compact disc tray of the machine, notched the chair back three reclining clicks and settled down. This is where it all has started, the concept album his brother had bought him when he was 14 years old – his first album and a slice of 1985. It all flooded back, it was a powerful sensation and, to his amazement, he remembered most of the lyrics.

'This is it,' Keith told himself as the tune slipped onto his favourite track, 'Mylo'. 'Ah – *I remember Toronto when Mylo when down, we sat and we cried on the phone, I never felt so alone, he was the first of our own.'*

Something grabbed Keith's foot and he let out a high pitched squeak – a little too high for a 39 year old man. The 1970's garden recliner folded under him.   The stranger in the room leapt backwards.

'Thought you were dead, man. I heard the music and thought this Marillion crap had made you kill yourself.'

Keith could only muster a singular response.

'You git, you absolute, gitty, git, git!'

Composing himself a little and still wrestling with the chair, Keith demanded, 'who the hell are you?'

'I'm Heggie, I live at the bottom of your garden. What are you doing in here man?'

After calling Heggie a 'git' once more, Keith declared, 'it is rule number one of this here listening studio that you don't creep up on people.'

'Studio, eh? Rules, eh? Nice set up,' Heggie said as he walked with a slow bounce around the shed, inspecting the compact discs, stereo equipment and the general ambience of the shed.

'Before you ask,' Keith said, as he struggled to get the elastic bit which held the cover in place over the top of the chair, 'this is a retro chair, designed to provide a minimalistic feel to the place.'

'But Marillion though......,' Heggie said, with a wince appearing on his face.

'Keith, its Keith.'

'But Marillion though Keith, that's a bit desperate isn't it. Surely you can do better than that!'

'My first album if you must know, broke the mould it did and still one of the finest concept albums, even today – I can adequately defend it. Anyway, less of that, how did you get in here?'

Heggie looked at the shed door and was just about to state the obvious when he thought better of it; after all, he was still technically an intruder at this point.

43

'I came through the hedge, man – from the other side,' raising his hand in a sweeping arc and using a cosmic voice. 'I was intervening in a titanic struggle between the azaleiers and the humble climbing rose; it all gets a bit nasty when that kicks off in June. The garden can be a tough place when you are a slow growing perennial. It was then when I heard the unmistakable, pained guitar of Mr. Stephen Rotheray, piercing my orchard and upsetting my orange pippins man, that's an apple to you Keith.'

'You seem to know a lot about Marillion for one who thinks they're pretty rubbish - having just named the lead guitarist,' Keith half asked.

'I met them on tour in Germany in 1983, their 'Script for a Jester's Tear' tour. Yeah, did some work setting up 'The Web' their official fan website. They were huge and I do like their stuff, I was only kidding you.'

Keith thought it would be a good time to release his Marillion related story.

'My mate Neil, who once played zips in a band called 'Sheep Dip' stole a crate of beer from Fish's garage when he lived in Gerrard's Cross.' Sensing that the story didn't quite cut it, Keith followed up with the one about nearly being run over by one of the Bee-Gees in his yellow Rolls Royce outside the Packhorse Pub, again, in Gerrard's Cross. Keith thought he had better leave it there.

'I was at Fish's house once, must have been about the same time. The band were practicing and running through a few new ideas for the next album. We had drinks on the patio and I do remember there being a distinct lack of beer,' Heggie said with a semi-sideways glance at Keith. 'Nice house, big pond – no fish though,' he chuckled.

44

'Here we are,' said Heggie, pulling Pink Floyd's Dark Side of the Moon album from Keith's pile. 'If you are going to do it right, start here – with all respect to Marillion. This album demands involvement! I went on tour with Floyd to North America. I spent some crazy days with them in the studio recording 'Meddle' which was released in October 1971 – probably not long after you were born Keith. The music press were split on that album – referring to either a soundtrack from a film that was missing or, as Rolling Stone, put it 'and exceptionally good album'. 'Echoes' apparently was the 'zenith the Floyd have been striving for'.'

'Play an instrument then?' Keith enquired.

'Only the buffoon, which is really a no then, just helping out with the general mojo of the place. The management considered me to be an invigorating influence on the band. Ah, the recording studio, what a great place, only experience by the few. Behind the glass, making it happen, sitting back and just soaking up the raw music.'

Heggie's concentration returned to the present and he looked jolly as he spoke. 'And I see you are trying to re-create that scene here, in your very own shed. I'm liking it, man. Come on, let me have a go!' And with a twang of recliner elastic, Heggie was seated. He mumbled his way through the CDs, 'too manic, never heard of them, bit too cardigan for me….. Ah! The Specials 'eh. Good Coventry band. Formed in '77, you can really feel the grittiness of Coventry of the time in their music. One of the best acts to combine danceable Ska and rocksteady beat with punk's energy and attitude.'

Keith nodded and spoke. 'I can remember being absolutely transfixed to the TV, rooted to the spot when 'Ghost Town' came onto Top of the Pops, 1981, it was June and I had was just turned10 years old. I didn't think I would ever feel the same. These days I'm just loving their other stuff 'Nothing ever change' and 'Why'. Funny how you start off on one track and move onto liking their other stuff better, almost becoming disappointed with the track that led you to them because it was more commercial. It was difficult to get my head around racism back then, being only a youngster, but yet this mixed heritage band were singing about the stark reality and I couldn't see how society could ever work, but here we are. I'd like to think bands like The Specials, UB40 and that whole genre moved things along.'

'Yeah, we all have that Top of the Pops moment,' Heggie replied, 'for me it was Tracy Ullman singing 'Breakaway' into her hairbrush. Can still remember it today, wow, stirred me throughout the midriff that did! When music pushes the boundaries Keith and is new, it lends itself particularly well to the political statement.'

Heggie flicked through some more of Keith's CDs. 'Suede, not bad, the real heroes of Brit pop in my humble opinion. They cut a fine and clean image and paved the way for the rest of them - although I stand firmly in the middle between Blur and Oasis – that'll upset the Gallaghers I'm sure.' Heggie fingered the Prince Buster and Madness CDs. 'There is a real theme emerging here Keith.'

'Well yes, I suppose they are all a bit Ska-ish. Old-old Ska, old ska and more pop Ska.'

'More than that dear boy, Prince Buster, for me, is the most important figure of that time in developing Ska into rocksteady…. that's a slower way of dancing to Ska to you Keith. This paved the way for expediting reggae, although Prince stayed true to rocksteady because of his religious beliefs.   One of his rivals tried to stop him by dropping a lump on concrete on his head. Prince Buster was in hospital and found out this rival was telling everyone 'Prince Buster has gone mad!' On hearing this, he leapt from his bed and ran through the streets with his head bandages flapping in the wind shouting – 'if this is madness, then I'm filled with gladness!'   That's where Madness took their name from.   They paid homage to him in 'The Prince' – listen to the lyrics Keith ... *the man who set the beat...'*   The Specials covered a number of tracks including 'Too hot' and 'Enjoy yourself' and then so did so many others Keith. The man's a legend!

'Marvin Gaye Keith! A very wide range of musical tastes!   Ah Marvin, old Marvin, he announced his genius through this 1971 album 'What's going on' combining social commentary with an anti-Vietnam War stance. Marvin it is, and very fitting for this sunny day.'

'Marvin it is then,' Keith repeated, taking the CD from Heggie.

'Fire up the old ....,' there was a pause as Heggie squinted closely at the stereo. 'Yeah, fire up the Samsung 1300 then Keith and away we go!'

Track one filled the shed.   Heggie reclined Auntie Hazel's chair, the arms clicked a few times and he sprang back with a jolt.

'Nice,' Heggie smoozed, extracting a pair of sunglasses which has until now been buried in his mop of thick, dark, curly hair. Heggie pulled the sunglasses over his eyes with a slow and exaggerated movement.

Heggie was in good nick for his age Keith thought, one of those chaps that looked like he suited the age he was now. He looked like a fairly cool geezer and the years of the hinted at rock excess hadn't troubled his appearance. He was not wearing the get up you would expect from a full on gardening session; his was the garb of an old rocker. Black boots, size 10 as Keith could clearly see from the reclined figure, blue well worn jeans - but not ripped or torn and an ensemble of an expensive looking long sleeved red and blue patterned shirt, black hooded top with the sleeves cut off and a well worn leather waistcoat. It all looked in place and as if it had come in one piece from a gentleman rocker outfitters.

Keith stood there for a moment, experiencing the surreal. A 'lived in' rocker, who he knew nothing about apart from the odd sighting in the garden behind his, sat in Auntie Hazel's chair, listening to his music in his shed. Quite comfortable he was too! Keith thought he had better say something rather than stand their like a voyeuristic lemon. Keith opened his mouth but Heggie muttered 'magic' in a hedonistic manner so Keith felt himself suitably stopped and possibly about to breach rule number 1.

Keith stepped back into his garden. He looked for the hole in the hedge but couldn't see one. He tried parting the hedge in several places but couldn't really see a way through.

Once, when Keith was mending a tile on his roof he could see part of the property behind whence Heggie had come from - the orchard, the established grounds and a part of the house and it looked like a whopper. He had also seen Heggie lying in the border, just lying there gazing up at the sky, not moving a muscle.

Keith had a chuckle to himself, *'who would have thought! I have a man living at the bottom of my garden – and a rock star to boot!'* Keith went back into the house leaving Heggie to get on with it. He didn't see Heggie leave but in the late afternoon, he saw a note pinned to the side of the shed, it read:

'Thanks Keith – loved the shed experience. Might come again soon with my mate Marcus. Come through the hedge and up to the house if you want to. Munyana Banana, Heggie.'

.oOo.

This is Keith's mind. Cranial swelling has increased and I've now got pressure on the frontal lobes. This isn't good. Since Keith read that article about the size of frontal lobes and the link between size and addiction I've been trying to do the calculations. I think Keith's frontal lobes are larger than the average so there's not much room for a lot of inflammation. The addiction activity accounts for the relatively poor condition of the liver and lungs, rather than the impact we've suffered. At the moment I'm reading an epitaph.... 'Nice bloke, just couldn't stay off the addictives.'

Chapter 11

Marcus

From where he was working on his computer, Keith could see Heggie was in the shed. Heggie was busy moving Keith's nine-ply sheets of timber which had been laid up against the back of the shed for some time into the shed.

There was another man with Heggie, presumably this Marcus character. From a distance, Marcus looked a bit like Heggie. Keith entertained himself by thinking of the collective noun for a group of aging rock type people. A 'crash' – no, that was too obvious and they may get upset as being referred to as a group of rhino's. How about a 'rift'? or a 'wrinkle'? Keith chuckled to himself, yes, a 'wrinkle' would do.

Judging by Marcus' appearance, Keith thought that there must be a shop somewhere that sells a full suite of old style rocker gear.

Keith could see quite clearly that their discussions, probably about old times and high jinks, had been interrupted as Marcus lifted Auntie Hazel's chair into the air to get a better look at it. It looked like the chair was getting some fine respect. *'Yes, a very good example of early eighties utility garden wear,'* he thought they would be saying.

After a while, and thinking it would be a bit rude not to say hello to the people using his shed, Keith wandered down the garden. He was a bit nervous as he didn't feel he was all that comfortable hanging out with music types. Keith has only been to a few gigs. Apart from the dodgy ones at university, Keith had really only been to one, a Marillion gig at Wembley Arena. It was a good one however according to Keith as Marillion had since been voted in at 38th in the top 50 rock bands to see live. Keith and Ben had thought it would be a jolly good idea to get their faces pained like the jester on the front cover of the albums.

'Are you sure this is a good idea?' Ben had asked.

'Yeah, yeah, the jester has been with the band on their album covers since the beginning. Everyone knows the jester! It's a metamorphosis Ben, from his crude, maniacal and wild ways to the more mature and reasoned fellow that he is now. Look, here he is on the cover of 'The Great Cucumber Massacre' knife in hand, drooling, with the monocle covering one of his bloodshot, red eyes. And here he is again, lying on his bed on 'Fugazi', looking a bit forlorn and sick on his glass of wine. Here's 'Misplaced Childhood' and he's reasoning with himself and just leaving through the window. Here he is again at the end of the bar on 'Clutching at Straws' having now taken off his jester's outfit, he's obviously more comfortable with himself.'

The fact that the jester had left through the window and then taken off the harlequin outfit should have acted as a warning to Keith. When they got to Wembley Arena; they found the band and the crowd had moved on. They felt right fools being the only ones who had made that sort of effort. In fact, only one person recognised the significance of the facial attire enough to make a comment and that was a drunk in the toilet, who, between his vomits managed an 'oh yeah, I get it, nice one guys', so that didn't count.

Keith had managed to get backstage once to see Desmond Dekker at the Cheltenham University Summer Ball held at the Cheltenham racecourse. Keith would visit that fine racecourse for many years to come for the Cheltenham Festival, the pinnacle event of the horse racing jumps calendar, but on this occasion Keith was mixing with legends in the form of Desmond and what was left of the Aces.

He had waited ages at the stage door to see the band as he'd lost the rest of the drinking party he was with. Eventually he was ushered in to meet the band and after a brief 'hello' with what seemed a very nice group of exhausted musicians; he was out manoeuvred and outgunned by an extremely tall lady who declared in a very loud and gauche voice; 'You must remember me! I toured with Pauline Collins'. Keith thought *'oh, those heady days of Ska,'* as he slid slowly and disappointedly out of the backstage area. Keith felt inadequate again.

'Keith, Keith.' Heggie greeted Keith energetically and excitedly. He encouraged Keith with a 'come on into the studio'.

'How posh am I?' thought Keith, *'a man living at the end of my garden and a studio.'*

Heggie was sat on one side of the newly erected wooden ply sheet in the other one of the chair pair, being Uncle Sam's old recliner. The sheet was stood upright to provide some privacy to the 'guest' situated on the other side. Keith peered over.

'Marcus,' whispered Heggie pointing at the reclined figure, 'he just loves your chair!' There was no music blaring out and it appeared quite serene apart from the metallic, repetitive thud of bass and the odd tingle from the cymbals. In the chair, Marcus was fully reclined, moving his shoulders alternatively like some disco dancing dad.

'What's he listening to?' asked Keith, thinking it would be some legend from the 60's, steeped in majesty with a dark and woeful story surrounding their fall from grace and untimely death.

'The Pet Shop Boys – the one with Dusty, he loves that stuff.'

'I'd better say 'hi' then,' said Keith, feeling a bit better about his musical provenance if the Pets Shop Boys were on the playlist today.

'No way,' replied Heggie, 'rule number two of the studio – no interruptions during duende!'

And there it was, 'duende', the word clearly used in the industry - and Keith was in the know! A special word, probably used secretly and traded around in select, music orientated circles.

'I know that word,' Keith said with medium satisfaction. 'Oh, I so feel I understand this music thing and, get this Heggie, I now have two rules for my music listening studio!'

Keith peeked over the board again. Marcus certainly looked like he was in 'duende'.

'He's one cool cat,' Heggie whispered. 'I first saw him on the set of 'Easy Rider' in 1968. He was discussing a scene with the late, great Dennis Hopper. Marcus was financing part of the movie and was taking quite a 'hands on' role. Certainly, he was an advocate of the long handlebars on the bike. Man, he was telling Hopper how to act! Hopper was directing the movie as well so goodness only knows how Marcus had gotten into that position!'

'He does look a bit like Dennis Hopper and do you know Heggie, you look a bit like Jim Morrison.'

'Perhaps we are indeed those people, escaped from the public eye and now holed up in your shed, keeping it real.'

'Well you're very welcome 'Jim' and 'Dennis'. It's been a good day Heggie. I know about duende, I have a music listening studio complete with two rules and nine-ply timber board and Jim Morrison and Dennis Hopper using it. I don't think I can take any more on today so I'll leave you to it!'

Keith headed for the door but Heggie started up again. Heggie was a story teller and his story must be told.

'I met Marcus for the second time in the 'Chiquito Cizitio', that's the 'small sausage' bar to you Keith, down in Cuba. He was toasting off playing a major role in the success of Woodstock, the Aquarian Exposition, those three days of love and peace in White Lake, New York.

'He was sat in the shade of the veranda. In front of him he had a large jug of mohjito, a bottle of tequila with double worms and three packs of Marlborough full strength cigarettes. I didn't get the impression he was going anywhere for a while. Marcus recognised me from my on stage cameo with Hardy Woodpecker's band. Like your friend Neil played the zips, I played the canastas – I had one positive review in the NME you know.'

'The cowboy hat Marcus was wearing had the biggest brim you can imagine and although his face was shaded, I could still see his eyes were as bright and as clear as the Tijuana sky. It used to be the thing to do to catch some recovery time in Cuba after a really big one. Cuba is one beautiful place Keith, kissed by the same sultry sun as the rest of the Caribbean but most unlike it, if you catch my drift. It has 3,735 kilometres of coastline as well as rough, high ground rising up to the peak known as Pico Turquino at just over 2000 metres.

'The cantinesos, that's the top bar men of the country to you Keith, were telling Marcus about serving rum to Al Capone and Ernest Hemingway and that Frank Sinatra was sitting in the very seat that Marcus was sitting in. We got chatting about the gig and I offered Marcus one of the cigars I had bought from Vinales, the world's best dark tobacco rolled on the thighs of the women who worked there.

'We ate the best Cuban dishes, all influenced by the proximity to Africa and listened to traditional folklorico music as well as the more contemporary 'Afro Cuban All-Stars.

'Let's go in search of some culture,' Marcus declared once we finished the full range of drinks and we headed out on our wild travels. We made it about 20 meters before reaching La Floridita bar in Havana where we gorged on daiquiris and we were oozing with reckless abandon.

'We travelled for the rest of 1969 taking in the east of the country, including Oriente, where Fidel Castro was raised and visited the finca 'Las manacas' near Biran which was his childhood home. We went on through the Sierra Maestra mountains which was to become the rebel HQ 'Comandancia de la Plata' in the early 50's.

'Marcus recognised me for my magazma bringing qualities and we did a lot of business together. We travelled again in 1974 to Chile. We hooked up again with Hopper who provided the backing vocals to Bob Dylan in the Chilean Benefit Concert. After the gig, we headed out into town and Dylan took off his hat and started wearing this flowerpot on his head. Some dude nicked Dylan's hat and tore off through the market place, Hopper in pursuit. Those were high old times Keith. Me and Marcus then made our way up back to Los Angeles as we were trying to get something going.' Heggie was grinning ear-to-ear.

'We stopped by the Whisky A-Go-Go to take in some Doors before heading up to Sunset Strip to our hotel Chateau Marmont. The acid heads of the City of Angels were just starting to freak out and they were gradually becoming vagrants and making nuisances of themselves. The downside of happy abandon.

'The Marmont looms above Sunset Boulevard like Dracula's Transylvanian Castle looms above the pines of its surrounding forests. Since it was built in 1927, it has been inextricably linked to the profanities of excess. Marcus woke me up at 3am shouting 'Morrison's on the roof, he's trying to swing from the flagpoles!'

'I pulled on my pants and went down into the courtyard in the matchbox-sized wooden elevator. Marcus was in the courtyard.

'Morrison, you damn fool – get down here!' Marcus was shouting. 'Come along Morrison, I've got to get down to Hopper's room – he's got 50 girls there! That was the famous incident of Morrison using the eighth of his nine lives. What the reports don't tell you is about the English gent berating him for his actions and the same English gent complaining bitterly 'because of that loon, I've missed out on the (now famous incident of the) 50 girl party.

'Things quietened down a bit after that for all of about one morning. The hotel staff did their utmost to keep the grubby newspaper men away. The Marmont was all about discretion, although you wouldn't think that listening to the lyrics of the Eagles 'Hotel California', check out the album cover Keith; The Marmont.

'There was this big shot manager staying at the hotel. He was managing four of the biggest named musicians and bands of the time, four of the biggest names of all time actually now that I look back. He was so high on uppers and so down on downers he didn't know where he was! He was important in the music biz but generally you don't see those manager type guys

56

peacocking it around at hotels making buffoons of themselves, usually they are quiet and professional.

'This dude stood on the back of the springboard shouting 'I'm gonna do it man, I'm gonna fly, fly like and angel, right up to heaven and back. I'm gonna touch the sun everyone,' and with a tremendous 'boing' he flew off the springboard.

'Thirty people around the pool watched to see if he was ever going to come up, but he did, about five feet away from his trunks, and then a big old banger bobbed up. I have never laughed so much in my life. There it was, like a submarine surfacing, plink, plink.

'Two under reported side effects of chemical abuse Keith is an instantaneous and loose bowel movement and the creation of a tent like effect in one's swimming shorts. Although activities like losing one's shorts is the preserve of Mr. Bean films and doing bangers in pools is the stuff of norm for mental rocker type people, it's not what many high-end cool musicians in those days would have wanted to be associated with. You have got to remember Keith – we were all loving each other then, not pooping in each other's pools.

'Word started to get out about 'poolpoogate' and the press started to sniff around, if you excuse the pun Keith. John Belusi had overdosed the month before on speedballs so the press were hot for another story. We saw our opportunity to broker a deal with the pool felon. All Marcus and I had to do was to head the whole thing off with the press, just make it go away and he would make his four acts play at the festival we were trying to set up.

'I took the blame, it was all personally very embarrassing but there's no news in a magazma man disgracing himself. Funny how that poo in the pool changed the course of my life!'

As Marcus continued to enjoy the music and Heggie didn't appear to be stopping, Keith opened up one of his wooden folding chairs so he could sit down.

'Why did you do that, man?' Heggie asked.

'Do what?'

'Go 'ooohhh' as you sat down, like an oldie would do, they always do that.' Heggie mimicked 'oohh, aahhh, whoopa', rather enjoying the sound he was making.

'I do feel old sometimes Heggie, old for my 39 years. I'm finding I have to plan my journey to work around a halfway wee stop. On my way to Lewisham I have an opportunity between 8.12 and 8.15am to use the gents on platform B at Waterloo East before the train goes at 8.16am from platform A. The journey is two and a quarter hours so if I don't have a break, I will find myself in trouble. My knees crack a little as I walk up and down the escalators on the Underground and I can only get up the hill from the station on my bike in one go once in every five attempts.'

Heggie was studying Keith intently now and moved himself face to face.

'Do you look at yourself in the mirror sometimes and imagine what you might look like with a moooostache?' Heggie asked.

Keith nodded.

'Do you like summer shorts with the large, handy pockets?' he went on, raising his eyebrow ever so slightly.

'Possibly,' replied Keith.

'Do you think you might get an estate model when you change cars next time, an automatic?'

'I might not answer that one,' Keith said coyly.

'It happens,' Heggie said ruefully, leaning back in his recliner. 'Now take that man in there,' he said pointing over the timber sheeting, 'he was the man who put the 'roller' under the 'disco' throughout Europe. He had the biggest wheel orientated music venue on the continent. He energised the battlefields on the streets to mobilise the Ska movement and had five acts on Top of the Pops in one week. He rode the electronic sound wave, beckoning the dawn of the synthesizer and the electric light show. Although he lamented at the coming of the dancy-dancy acid house stuff, he did hold some of the biggest outings for the ravers across the fields of Essex. He mercilessly pursued money, orchestrating some of the pivotal events in latter day music history.'

'What does he do now?' Keith asked.

'He generally picks up a few groceries for his wife, runs some errands, mooches around - that sort of thing. He's slowed down a bit. He has a bit of fun but do you know Keith, he misses being in the thick of it. It happens to us all.' Heggie's voice was tinged with lament. 'You've got your family,' Heggie went on, sensing he had brought the whole place down too much.

'It's an old cliché, but yes, I know they are my biggest adventure,' replied Keith, trying to avoid any sensitivities around kids as he hadn't yet established anything about Heggie's home life.

'Don't be like Lennon,' Heggie went on. 'I read in the paper that Julian has to go to auctions to get memories of his father. Not sure if that was because he wasn't around much or he was so for other people.'

'I'm here, I'm with them, I do the right things, they love me, they tell me I'm a great dad, but I don't think I am. I can't quite put my finger on it. Why don't I think I come up to the mark?'   The silence that followed allowed deep analysis by the two of them. *I think it's because I'm killing myself with the cigarettes and the alcohol,'* thought Keith'. 'I'll leave you,' said Keith.

He rose and put on the most enormous granny like performance to cover his shame and sadness. 'I'm off to see my turf accountant; I'm going to make my fortune this afternoon at Chepstow. A 'Yankee' feels appropriate' he said, trying to lighten the mood.

'Ah, a combination of 11 bets 'eh?' Heggie replied.

'You like the horses then?'

'Never had a bet.'

'That surprises me for one who seems to know a bit about Yankees.'

'I did some mind and music therapy on a horse once, thoroughbred, tricky fella. Liked listening to 'Dire Straits' and a stable of his own. The stable lads were always talking about their bets; all I can remember is that a Yankee consists of 11 bets. I was only there for a short while, the horse calmed down once he got his dose of 'Brothers in Arms' every night piped into his box. Tell me more about betting one day Keith will you?' Heggie asked, 'and Keith,' Heggie said softly as Keith was stepping out of the shed door 'thanks for all this – I'm having a great time. You don't mind me using the shed do you? I've got some more visitors coming.'

As Keith ambled back up the garden and into his house he wondered who on earth Heggie would have in the shed next.

Resolute and with a fully charged children's MP3 player, Keith set off to join the ranks of the earphone brigade. Ford had loaded some more of Keith's collection onto the device. The morning seemed extra bright in anticipation of this musical journey. Keith did his final checks – train ticket: check, wallet: check, second wallet to give away to robbers if approached: check, watch, office pass, tissues and water bottle: check, check, check. Set MP3 to random play. Departure time 06:40 hours, insert earphones.

First track – Keane, 'Everything's changing' took Keith down Clare Road, turning into Blacksmith's Lane, crossing over the High Street to bus stop, 06:44 hours.

Keith took his headphones out to talk to the small Italian looking chap who always waited at the bus stop, smoking heavily; it would be rude not to exchange pleasantries.

'Morning,' said Keith.

'Morning.'

'You alright?'

'Yeah, you?'

'Yep, I'm alright. How's things?'

'Same old, same old, you know.'

'Yep. Good, the bus is early.'

The first bus through the village was a single decker, usually late with one passenger, a lady asleep on the third seat in on the left. Keith had never seen her face.   Her cheap leggings stretched across the disproportionate large backside which stuck out into the aisle with short, broad legs attached led him to conclude she was female.

Keith felt he had time for another track in the six minutes the bus took to get to the station so he clicked onto the next track. Keane's 'Somewhere only we know' with its mellowing tunes warmed him as the sun flickered on his face through the trees and the dirty bus window. Some wag had chiselled some of the letters from the bus sign to make a rude word.

'Large coffee please Lesley.' Keith placed his money on the cabin counter at the train station platform and took the lukewarm brown liquid to the accompaniments table to cheer it up with some milk and sugar. The cold milk on offer made the brown liquid even colder.

The 07:01 hours train was punctually late by the usual two minutes but there was no time to listen to another complete track so Keith allowed the earphones to dangle coolly around his neck.

Keith kept his eyes on the track. He liked to watch the training coming round the corner from Wendover. The track was straight for around 600 meters before sweeping gradually to the left before it was obscured by the steep banks and incumbent trees on each side a mile or so up the track. The visual image just screamed 'adventure' to Keith; the substance of childhood books. He felt more people should look out for the train – it seemed such a pleasurable thing to do.

Seat secured, which was not always a guaranteed thing given the 7:01 was a fast service to London and therefore a shorter service, Keith nudged the earphones back in. He clicked past 'Big fish, little fish, cardboard box' and 'The Purple People Eater' for, although entertaining, they were Ford's selection.

By Amersham Keith was listening to the bubbling melody of Lynyrd Skynyrd's 'The Seasons' and the sun shone full into his face so he could almost imagine himself in Florida, US. He'd always had an affinity to Southern US hard rock. He dreamed of being at 3164 Jackson Highway, Sheffield, Alabama at the Muscle Shoals Sound Studio when this stuff was recorded. He liked the idea that a group of musicians set this

thing up and called the studio after their group –
The Muscle Shoals Sound Rhythm Section. You
can go anywhere with things if you are in charge.
That ordinary building was stuff of magic. That
ordinary building has been incorporated into the
US National Register of Historic Places. Keith
wanted to do something like that. Keith wanted to
leave a bit of a legacy.

As the train glided past Chalfont and Latimer,
The Stone Roses were still amazing Keith with the
complexity and boldness of 'Fools Gold'. Keith
could understand why a 16 year old Liam
Gallagher in the audience of a Stone Roses gig
would be inspired to start a band.

As he passed Chorleywood, the Stones were
emotionally dominating the whole of Keith's mind
with 'Wild Horses' – was there ever a song which
conjured up lament and the opportunity of life as
much as this?

At Neasden the train slowed a little as the line
became more congested however this seemed to
fit the mood of the British trip hop Massive Attacks'
'Unfinished Sympathy' – going somewhere with a
purpose, *'Hey, hey, hey ahyah!'*.

The train was once again gliding through
tunnel 1 and 2 approaching Marylebone. Led
Zeppelin did 'Whole lotta love' from the 1976
offering 'The Song Remains the Same', taken
from the first three nights at New York's Madison
Square Garden 1973 North American Tour. Keith
arrived at platform four, 7:42 am, just as Robert
Plant wailed his final wail.

It only seemed fitting to fill the short walk to
Baker Street Tube station and the six stops on the
Jubilee Line tube to Southwark (for Waterloo East)
with the whole of Metallica's 'Ride the Lightening'
album. Now, you may wonder why Keith,
appreciator of American hard rock, had become

63

so fond of Metallica's thrash metal that he dedicated a large part of his journey to it, particularly given the very thrash content and nature of the tracks:

The opener, 'Fight Fire with Fire' states the eye for an eye attitude, revenge and Armageddon, resulting in the end of the world. The next offering 'Ride the Lightning' concentrates on the misery of the criminal justice system; the lyrics are written from the perspective of someone who is waiting for death by electrocution. 'For Whom the Bell Tolls' follows and is based on the Ernest Hemingway novel by the same name - about the horror and dishonor of modern warfare. The chromatic introduction is a bass guitar augmented with distortion and a wah-wah pedal but sounds like an electric guitar.

'Fade to Black' suggest contemplation of suicide. Guitar players might pick up that the acoustic intro has 12 strings but others may spot it has no conventional chorus. Trapped Under Ice – imagine waking up in a cryonic state – bit of a downer, waiting, helpless, doomed terror. 'Creeping Death' hits a Biblical note describes the Plague of Death (Exodus 12:29).

Written during the fall of 1983, the songs were recorded at Sweet Silence Studios, Copenhagen. Due to the signing of a new record deal, Metallica released the album twice in 1984, through Megaforce on 27 July and Elektra Records on 19 November.

Keith liked it because it featured the thrash genre's first power ballad in 'Fade to Black'. It included melody, musical intelligence and harmonious complexity. Rolling Stone said 'that the band's sophomore record was another big step forward from their groundbreaking debut album'.

With the elevation sensation of rising two flights of stairs and two lengthy escalators into the sunshine of platform B of Waterloo East, The Manic Street Preachers' 'Suicide is painless' was very apt. Whilst having a convenience stop in the gents on Platform B, for safety reasons, Keith took the earphones out, again, nonchalantly leaving them to drift freely over his shoulders. Keith transferred to Platform A at 8:11am so there was just enough time to squeak in Paulo Nitini's invigorating 'Candy'.

It had been a lovely journey. On the return leg, Keith did the same and listened to more music, but this time accompanied by a can of pop and a Drifter chocolate bar.

Chapter 12

In Pursuit of the Ultimate 400 Meters Freestyle, Part 2 (The Test)

The Handy Cross sports centre sits next to the M40 in Buckinghamshire. The fairly unusual design of tall glass panels on three of the four sides of the swimming pool creates a light and airy feel. It gets hot in the summer but there is nothing quite like the look of the pool when the sun is shining on top of the water.

Keith stood at the deep end of the pool. This was his home pool. Today, he was to race over Alan's suggested 400 meters front crawl. The longer distance was about right – it was his event and he knew how to swim it.

He thought through the race. Out solid and steady for the first 100 meters. Middle 200 meters push the pace to keep the momentum up and keep the time splits steady, adding more effort every 25 meters. The lungs would be burning at around 250 meters but the end would be in sight. Hold for the last 100 meters, stretch, power through at the end of the stroke, keep the stroke steady. Fast final turn, bounce off the wall and then to the legs for the last 50 meters. This was his own race, he would swim it his way. The other competitors didn't matter – the old lady doing side stroke in lane 2 didn't matter, the breast stroking geriatric who had left his prosthetic leg on the side wasn't a concern. In fact, that afternoon, the public session at the pool was rather quiet.

It had been 20 or so long years since Keith had swam competitively.

The first 200 meters went well. Keith stopped after 250 meters to loosen his trunks and tighten

66

his goggles. The old shoulders were still in need of careful treatment. After 350 meters, Keith got cramp in both legs, which is not conducive to high level training and unhelpful when you try and get out of the pool.

The young lifeguard was very helpful in this latter respect, following his initial reluctance to come down from his high chair. Keith had paid £5.15 as a non-member adult to humiliate himself.

'See that man over there, the one in the shower?' one of the flowery hat swimmers was sure to be saying to the other one.

'What, the one with the lovely stroke?'

'Still holds a club and County record for his 1500 meters front crawl he does. Won the Midland Districts and had a GB senior mens' top 10 ranking he did.'

''Let himself go a bit hasn't he.'

Chapter 13

Mr Fuzz, One Stressed out Cat

Keith returned home and poured himself a very large glass of red wine. There was enough of the evening left for a good walk around the garden and perhaps even a sit down in the last rays of the sun. Summer was in full flight, the ground had become hard and there was a real warmth to the air.

Keith stepped out into his garden to take a few minutes for himself. He sat with his face to the sun, took his sunglasses off so he could feel the full force of what was left of the bright day on the back of his eyes. He took a sip of his red wine and the flavour seemed to fill his lungs as well as his throat. *'Lovely,'* he thought to himself. He imagined he was on holiday, Sanlucar sounded nice – that would do – the brilliant sun, clear waters, unspoilt beaches, large shady terraces and a pool where he could blister in the sun. The local tavernas were sure to come alive at night and he was just a stone's throw from the lost city of Atlantis.

Keith couldn't sit down for long, he never could do. Guilt would get him. He would have to walk about and get involved in things and then after the opportunity to sit was gone, he would regret not just sitting and relaxing.

Heggie was at the shed when Keith got to that part of the garden and he was beckoning Keith like a mad-un. Heggie was agitated and excited.

'Sorry,' said Heggie, 'I was going to give you a break from my visitations but this is an emergency! We've got one stressed out cat!'

68

'How come it's 'we' now you've got a problem?'

'He's the fuzz you know.'

'A Fuzzy Cat? Well what's it doing here?'

'Ah,' said Heggie, 'I called him. The most terrible thing has happened – someone got into my garden and threw some of my laxton superb through my shed window!'

'Threw your what? And you've got your own shed?'

'Yeah, it's a mess man! Apples, laxton superb is my favourite apple, sweet, good eater with flecked green and red skin. I'm devastated.' Heggie shuddered as if reliving the moment he had come across the broken shed window, rather missing Keith's point about Heggie having his own shed. 'And my tortoise has gone missing. I called the Police. They really are taking it very seriously – they've sent round a Detective Inspector no less. You can count on the British Bobby – hard job. In the world of policing, the L.A.P.D., that's the Los Angeles Police Department to you Keith have a reputation for being good, but they weren't interested when someone tried to steal my Hummer and drove it through my tomato patch and into my jacuzzi. Beef tomatoes they were, biggest I've ever grown.'

Keith hadn't ever invited the translations from Heggie and it was becoming a bit of a theme, but he thought it was quite endearing and eccentric, so he didn't mind really.

'He's so stressed out,' Heggie continued, 'he's got two ticks! He does this,' – Heggie jerked his head to one side, 'and this,' giving a good impression of a chicken flapping one wing. Heggie looked a lot like Keith's best man's dancing style at his wedding – now referred to in legend as the 'Peter funky chicken.'

'I said to him, man, you just gotta take time for yourself! But he reckons he can't – he's got targets and he's only got a crime clear up rate of 33.7% and, worse than that, he's got to drive a marked Ford Fiesta so that he's 'high vis' in the community. The things they make our police do these days, it's just cruel.'

'Well, let's have a look at him then.'

'Oh yeah, right, he's in here. I have him listening to 'Tijuana brass plays the summer of 1965. It's a new invention to the studio – I now control from here the feed of the music, I'm now selecting what our guests hear, that's if they want me to. He's probably down there in Alicante, on the beach in his Hawaiian shirt and shorts.' Heggie gave Keith a sideways glance, 'shorts with large pockets. It will do him some good - restoration for the inner man!'

Keith peered over the board. The DI looked pinched, awkward and was probably in need of a whole decade of Tijuana brass rather than just 1965. He was balding but covered it with a long comb-over of thin mousy hair. His moustache was thick and bristly with flecks of grey and the light brown suit was very Detective Inspector. All he was missing was a radio or mobile phone clipped to his belt.

'He looks like he has most of the component parts of the crime fighting phenomena that Prestwood requires. I'm sure that he'll have it solved in no time. He has a nice thick jacket and a bit of stubbly tiredness going on around his chin.'

'Probably a crossword expert with a huge drink problem and a very difficult and dysfunctional private life,' chipped in Heggie.

'Well it looks like you have him nicely settled and receiving some inner sanctuary, I'm sure he will be better for it. I hope he rapidly gets to the bottom of this most absolutely heinous crime to give you some comfort Heggie.'

'Ah, thanks Keith. It's all a bit too traumatic for me!'

'I'm going to leave you now Heggie, I wouldn't want to impede investigations, I'm sure one has to act quickly to recover wandering tortoises but I am sorry to hear about your apples. Nice hat stand,' Keith said as he left the shed.

'Thanks for noticing!' Heggie cheerily called after him.

Keith saw the stressed out DI a few days later at Great Missenden train station. It was the ticks that first made Keith notice him. He appeared be to guarding the telephone box, but he was, on closer examination, having a crafty cigarette, hand cupped over the ciggie like a naughty schoolboy. His chicken wing was still going, but what was this? His head was jerking more frequently, like he was doing a restrained head-banging session, encompassing the two ticks he already had. He was grooving, yes, that was it!

As Keith approached on his bike he could see blue cables coming from the DI's ears. The man looked positively transformed. Keith was obviously staring too much and the DI clocked him and became self conscious. They had never been introduced so the DI wasn't aware that it was Keith's shed he had been in. Keith had heard from Heggie that the DI had been given his notice for an early retirement and that the Fuzzy Cat was angry, very angry.

Chapter 14

In Pursuit of the Ultimate 400 Meters Freestyle, Part 3 (The First Judgement Set)

Keith stood at the end of Lambeth's finest deck level 25 meter, 6 lane pool in the Brixton Leisure Centre. The South Bucks and Berkshire County record holder adjusted his baggy trunks to make sure they adequately covered the expanse of his backside. He needed a new pair.

It was a nice pool with three lanes dedicated to lunchtime swimmers. The fast lane was of course clogged up with breaststrokers – six in total, so Keith selected the medium lane which only had one person in it doing fast front crawl.

After a nice warm up of a mix of front crawl and double armed backstroke – old school style, Keith was ready for his 'judgement set'. This would allow him to chart his progress the more he swam. He had chosen five x 100 meters front crawl with a variable rest interval so that he could get some clear water, he could swim in between the other swimmers in the lane and not make a nuisance of himself with his thrashing about.

The judgement set started well enough with a time of 1 minute and 20 seconds for the first 100 meters. That was good enough for the first go – he would reduce his time down on the remaining with a blast on the final one. The second 100 meters was good, 1 minute 18 seconds and still feeling okay. The third shaved another two seconds off, getting a bit more puffed out.

The fourth was completely interrupted by a new swimmer who, it seemed, waited until Keith was just going into his turn at 50 meters before pushing off right in front of him. Although Keith was suffering at this stage, he still made it in 1 minute 25 seconds, but call it 1 minute 17seconds due to the traffic.

Just as Keith was about to start his final 100 meters, the aqua aerobics session started and a wave of people who has amassed at the side of the pool now entered it in one tsunami of flesh. The fast lane was rapidly filled with the most magnificent collection of portly people imaginable in one place. The water was somewhat displaced, as were the six fast lane breaststrokers who joined the medium lane. Eleven swimmers in such a confined space meant that Keith was unable to complete his judgement set. He got out.

Keith collected his stuff from the locker; he was pleased it was still there. It had been worth it, three swims now in as many weeks and the subsidised rate of £3.65 was very good value for money on the whole. It made the precarious walk through Electric Avenue and the market place and the long queue behind the gentlemans' over 50 keep fit exercise class worth it.

'Did you swim this week?' asked Alan.
'Yes, managed to do a session.'
'How'd it go?'
'It went great for the first 15 minutes and then someone dropped a piano on my back. Lots of traffic in the lane and you wouldn't believe me if I told you about the sights from the Aqua Aerobics lesson. I'm going to invest in a pair of dark goggles so I can't see so much under the water.'

Chapter 15

Record Scouts and Physiatrists

Keith was busy deadheading some plants he had forgotten the name of. He wasn't quite sure how far down he should pinch the dying stems, so he did a random height on each one. He also thought it might be easier to use some secateurs.

'Keith, Keith, come quick,' came the cry from the end of the garden. It was Heggie. 'It's that cat!'

'Which cat? Marcus the cool cat or Fuzzy Cat, the stressed out just about to lose his job cat? Oh no! I hope he hasn't done anything stupid in my shed!' shouted Keith now getting a wriggle on down the garden. 'I can just see the headline in tomorrow's Buck's Free Press:

'SACKED DI FOUND DEAD IN GARDEN LISTENING STUDIO' *weird circumstances surround the discovery of a sacked DI who was found dead in a garden 'music listening studio'....*

They had put the music listening studio in inverted commas as people wouldn't understand. Keith felt slightly mocked by the press coverage that he had just made up. The article would continue...

'*...former Detective Inspector, Fuzzy Cat, 53, was found dead last night in Keith T Armstrong's garden shed. Two men have been arrested in connection. The acting DI, Gunter Hunter said in a statement... tragedy... when good intentions go wrong... no stone... sympathy to family... appears linked to a series of apple incidents and a tortoise...'*

74

'In there!' Heggie wailed, having lost all control now. Keith was brave and peered round the door, holding his breath; after all, he had never seen a dead-un before. What would he see? Blood, strangulation, a sad picture of a fallen crime fighter trussed up in ladies lingerie? The unusual application of a variety of fruit?

'That's Mrs. Brown's cat you damn fool. Mrs Brown of next door!'

'Well, get it out, ugly creature! It's the eyes! That cat looks at me when I'm in the garden,' cried Heggie. 'Get it out please, I've got Amelia coming.'

'Ah well, in normal circumstances, I wouldn't usually bother – I'd leave it settled in Auntie's chair, but as you have Amelia coming, I'll get it out straight away! Come on Mandu,' Keith said, calling the cat and rubbing the end of his fingers together like he had something interesting on offer.

'Is that its name, 'Mandu'?' asked Heggie, not really wanting anything to do with the cat but was slightly surprised Keith was on first name terms.

'I've no idea,' replied Keith, 'probably, Cat-Mandu is its show name, not a bad looking cat that. Come on Mrs Brown's cat. Oh, nice lamp Heggie.'

'Thanks for noticing.'

With only seconds to spare, the cat was successfully shooed and Amelia appeared, totally inappropriately dressed in her London fashion and high heels for squeezing through hedges.

'She works for a major record company,' whispered Heggie 'as a scout for new talent – totally highly strung! I meet with her to get her head back together, 'reframing and refocusing' she calls it. To be honest, I don't know what to do with her – I just don't seem to understand these new breed of agents, it seemed so much simpler in my day.'

'Now who's getting old?' chuckled Keith, looking down at Heggie's shorts, 'let me see the size of those pockets.'

'Hi guys,' was Amelia's introduction which didn't seem to match the formulaic London appearance.

'Well I wouldn't be able to pick her out of a crowd at Marylebone station in the 'spot the record scout' competition,' Keith whispered back to Heggie.

'Oh, it is soooo rural here. Had a nightmare, a nightmare you know. Hundreds of school kids got on the train at Amersham. Ugh! Noisy lot they were too and I got thumped by a guitar. Then there wasn't a taxi in sight at Missington station.'

'Miss-en-den,' Keith said, 'it's Great Missenden,' getting a touch of the patriotics about his fair station. 'Aren't those kids your target audience? Think of the raw talent, unplundered in this.... rural location'. Keith's comments seemed to go over Amelia's head as she simply gawped at him.

'It's a good job the nice man in the bookies gave me a lift up the hill. Very pleasant...' Amelia trailed off and got a misty look in her eyes '...rugged, a bit dangerous...' She stopped abruptly; realising that she was speaking out loud something that she thought was only going on in her head. 'It's quite posh though around here isn't it?' Amelia continued. 'Even the rubbish left on the streets is posh. I noticed that you have Ginsters pie wrappers, gin and tonic cans and M&S bags as litter whereas we in London only get the yellow polystyrene take away boxes and extra strong beer cans. Even the Home Counties alcoholics are posh. They're plump through their economic status, with the effects hidden by holiday tans and Armani sunglasses. Good middle class alcoholism cared for in big homes. My local alcoholic is tanned through exposure to the weather and thin through a lack of healthy food and a diet of rolled up cigarettes.'

Keith was unsure what had generated this tirade against alcoholics, possibly the dark rings around both his and Heggie's eyes however, the initial exchange had left Keith feeling he wanted more from a record scout and agent, at least one who was in touch with, rather than disgusted by, the local 'yoof'.

Although he didn't know anything about the industry, he felt he agreed with Heggie – the business had certainly changed. Keith thought he could make a good stab at being a record scout – that all seemed pretty sexy and he thought he could do it, yeah, he could cut it in big business.

'You might want to go back to basics,' was Keith's offering to Heggie as he watched Amelia stagger towards the shed, briefcase in one hand and coffee cup in the other. 'May I suggest 'Take That' as an item for your musical menu?'

'Great idea, thanks for that,' said Heggie.

'Nice curtains Heggie,' Keith called as he headed back to his house.

The note that evening read:

'Thanks Keith, I think she got it! It is best to cut chrysanthemums one inch from the base, with sharp secateurs, to stop infection. Munyana Banana, Heggie'

'Now I'm getting gardening advice from Jim Morrison,' Heggie thought to himself. *'Surely*

77

Amelia knew it already – how did she get the job in the first place?' Keith mused, *'the first question at interview should be 'what is 'duende'? That would weed them out!'*

Amelia was the first of two visitors that week to the shed. Keith was lamenting the galloping past of the good weather, just yards from his chair tucked up to the computer. Keith had a full day's work ahead of him. The sun shone brilliantly and by mid afternoon, the wafts of warm air were puffing into the room laden with the smell of newly cut grass and the citrus scent from the fir trees. Keith was sure that some rotter had sparked up a barbecue just to make the idea of him missing out on the day even more unbearable.

Keith had been sidetracked by a mid morning show on TV. A warring couple had completed a DNA test and it was great news that that the child was the partners so the kissing of the nanny incident was all forgotten. Monumental moments in the lives of those seeking to be stroked were played out on the screen before the nation. Life changing news was read from cards as if the host was announcing the winner of the 3.30 at Chepstow. Duncan from Chelmsford just couldn't trust Trix anymore and it was messing him up - and when she went out with her friends 'it was like rubbing a spoon into the wound.'

Keith felt grateful that he had none of that type of hardship or conflict in his life. It was truly a different world, but it was, he feared, becoming an increasing characteristic in society. *'Magic stuff though,'* thought Keith, *'well worth 35 minutes of anyone's time!'* The only section of this show that seemed not to be the preserve of the chavs and lowlifes was those wrestling and denying old alcohol addiction and it made for unpleasant viewing and gave Keith an ache in his liver.

Having now lost the thread of his work, Keith mooched around the house for a bit. Gazing out of the patio doors, he could see Heggie at the end of the garden. He was pretending to be interested in the bit of ground that was shaded by the trees, deep in needle drop which created a permanently dry area where only a few ferns had managed to get a foothold. Keith didn't know Heggie that well at all, but he knew him well enough that he wanted to talk. Heggie was too polite though to loom up at the window, uninvited.

'Hi Heggie, what's going on?'

Heggie was his usual animated self.

'I've an old college friend coming down to stay for a few days – thought I would show her the studio man, if that's all right with you?'

'That's fine, but 'the studio' is a bit grand Heggie don't you think, she'll be disappointed'.

'The physical manifestation of the studio is all but relative Keith. Daphne will see it as the haven it is! A haven for the tortured soul of Fuzzy Cat, an invigorating place to recharge and reframe Amelia, a place of enjoyment for Marcus as well as being a great social venue.'

By this time, Heggie was sweeping at the floor of Keith's shed with a long handled broom and dustpan set he must have bought himself. This was unusual because it wasn't undertaken very often, well never, and not by the guy who lived at the end of the garden. The yellow pan and brush on the end of the sleek sticks didn't seem to suit Heggie.

'Royalty is she Heggie? Why all the fuss, you mad cleaning lady?'

'She's now an eminent psychologist,' Heggie replied, 'I just want her to enjoy herself, and I suppose, want her to see the value in this as I do,' he said gesturing to the shed in which they stood. 'I thought I would lead her in with some Bob Dylan and then rekindle the old college memories with some Jefferson Airplane. We used to go and see Grace Slick perform whenever we could and Daphne always got invited backstage. The bands loved talking to her – on the road it can he a harsh and gruelling place.'

'I could imagine it can be quite lonely with lots of opportunities and time for deviations and temptations,' said Keith, thinking about how he often filled his 55 minute train journey from London with gin and tonic.

'A couple of minutes talking to Daphne always raised their spirits. We used to go to all the after gig performances, we had a wild time and we were always welcomed. Daphne just seemed to be recognised as a bright flame beacon in the darkness for these performing types. Therapy of the mind, although extremely different, can actually have pretty similar results to the chemically induced state of mind. Think about it Keith.

'In fact, if it wasn't for Daphne, Hendrix wouldn't have played Monterey. Although Hendrix was popular in Europe, the Experience's first US single, 'Hey Joe', didn't reach the Billboard Hot 100 chart on its release on 1 May 1967. Their fortunes improved when McCartney recommended them to the organizers of the Monterey Pop Festival. He insisted that the event would be incomplete without Hendrix, whom he called "an absolute ace on the guitar", and he agreed to join the board of organizers so long as the Experience performed at the festival in mid-June. It was a big gig. Daphne walked him through his own mind that night and he realised he

80

could do just about anything. The set ended with Hendrix destroying his guitar and tossing pieces of it out to the audience. She didn't realise that night though he had some lighter fuel with him and thank goodness it was only the guitar that got burnt. I'm interested in getting a psychologists view on this shed Keith – why I think it seems to work so well.'

'Well it's all good Heggie, you carry on. I'm pleased that it's getting a bit of a clean if the truth be told. I've got to get back to my work but may I complement you on the nice side table.'

'Thanks for noticing Keith. I stopped short of a doily.'

'That's right Heggie, keep it raw, keep it real!'

'Pop down tomorrow Keith if you can, I'd like you to meet Daphne.'

Keith had arranged his day so he could be at home and Heggie was just as animated as Keith thought he would be when he came through the hedge. Heggie's arms were like wind-mills one minute and then he was bowing low the next. Heggie gestured towards the shed, encouraging Daphne in and she seemed game to enter. Keith had a belly laugh, 'the Queen and the jester'.

Keith was keen to get down there to watch Heggie some more but really he wanted in on the psychologists report; on Heggie and the studio. Keith fidgeted as he gave them some time to settle but he also felt like he wanted some answers, not knowing quite what the questions were. Poor old psychologists! The client expectations of getting answers to the undefined questions. Keith set off. He knocked politely on his shed door and waited.

'Come on in Keith,' called out Heggie, 'it's your shed!'

Keith was surprised to see Heggie in the 'listening' chair, which was not the way he had imagined it.

'Hello Daphne, I'm Keith, pleased to meet you. Well, what's the verdict?'

'Verdict?' Heggie and Daphne said together.

'Yes, what's so magical about my shed that it lures in the tormented and can calm the most agitated?'

'Client confidentiality I'm afraid Keith,' replied Daphne. 'I'm only joking' she said, sensing he was immediately deflated.

'I think it's all things to all people,' she went on. 'We all enjoy different things and different aspects of those things. Take you for example Keith, I would imagine it is partly about rediscovering music after not listening to it for a while, your indulgence, time to yourself after the commitment to your children and family. You are also probably appreciating the music more now that you are, 39 is it? In here you are safe, you won't be snuck up on and as you have taken yourself out of the house and into the shed you don't feel so guilty if you miss the doorbell. Technology may have passed you by in some respects, but in here it is not a problem as your Samsung 1300 fits the surroundings beautifully and it is of no challenge or frustration to you. If you really had to push me then I would say it is about you and Heggie creating and owning something, perhaps even fulfilling something that you perceive as missing in your life, but may actually not be.'

'Wow, that is impressive. How can you possibly tell all that just from me standing here for a few minutes?'

'I can't Keith, Heggie told me all about it!'

Heggie roared with laughter. 'I hope you don't mind dear boy, after all, you are amongst friends here.'

They all spent a pleasant hour or so enjoying the reclusiveness of the shed. Daphne had brought some home made lemonade which was rather a fitting refreshment to enjoy tales of skinny dipping and champagne towers in penthouses stretching across cities on each continent. It did really feel like a club.

Chapter 16

In Pursuit of the Ultimate 400 Meters Freestyle, Part 4 (Three Sessions in One Week and One Dry Land Activity Over Indulgence)

Monday lunchtime. Keith stood at the end of the pool in the Stevenage Leisure Centre. He fumbled to find the cord of his trunks from under his burgeoning mid-drift. This temporary inconvenience mattered not; he held a club record for over 20 years.

The Stevenage pool must have been one of the first 25 meter pools built in the country. It was old and was likely to have been constructed as part of the new town development. More importantly; it was quiet which allowed for a decent swim.

His only gripe was that they had double width lanes so swimming around in a large circle was a bit disorientating. Call Keith old fashioned but he liked to swim in a fairly straight line - the wide lanes and deep diving pit made it seem like Keith was swimming in the sea and he frequently lost his sense of direction.

The judgment set went well reducing from a 1 minute 20 seconds down to 1 minute 14 seconds. The green shoots of recovery were in evidence.

A magnificent lunchtime swim, all internal organs and muscles sufficiently worked. Keith felt amazing. The quiet pool and the heavily subsidised price of £3.15 made it well worth being battered by the crutch wielding, Iceland bag carrying participants queuing up in reception for the free chair exercise and sauna session being laid on by the Local Authority.

Wednesday morning. Keith stood at the end of the Chiltern pool in Amersham. He used to swim here. He used to be like one of the Amersham Swimming Club squad members who were thrashing up and down in lanes one to three. He eyed the three remaining lanes. Nearest the wall was the priority disabled, eight people in the fast lane and two people in the medium lane.

He knew that the Amersham swimming squad members would view him as he had viewed old boys some 20 years ago 'sad old boy – heat one, lane one'.

Keith toyed with the unravelling hem of his swim cossie whilst he made his lane choice. If only they knew he was pretty good himself once. *'Yep, used to do six 1,500 meter sets in a three hour session. Used to be 10 s 6lb racing weight. You can eat anything you want when you were training nine sessions a week.'*

He chose lane two, the medium lane and jumped in. The bow wave he created made it across into lanes one and three, even with the anti wave lane rope. Keith bobbed up underneath the lane rope, caught his fingers between the plastic circles on his first stroke and then hit his heels on the trough during his first turn; not the best of starts.

As it was busy in the lane, he skipped his judgement set in favour of a more plodding 'Hungarian Rep' starting with a 100 meters, then 200 meters, 300 meters and then back down again to the 100 meters. It was more of an endurance set with regular rest times and conducive to a busy pool. The longer distance would do him some good on the stamina side of things.

The pool emptied and the club swimmers got out. With some clear water, Keith embarked on a very ambitious set of 20 x 75 meters front crawl with 15 seconds rest in between. That would set things up nicely - lots of mileage in the bank as it were.

After the set, Keith sat on the side and stretched his legs whilst he recovered. A most concerned lifeguard enquired about his health.

'I'm fine, really,' Keith reassured him. He wouldn't go away.

Gladys, the octogenarian swimmer in lane two finished her lap and asked Keith if he was okay.

'No really, I'm fine. Thank you.'

'You just look a bit red deary, that's all.'

The lifeguard remained close to Keith until he got up and went to change. 'Thought you might be havin' a heart attack mate.'

Thursday lunchtime. Keith stood at the end of the Ladywell Leisure Centre swimming pool, home of Saxon Crown Swimming Club the rather faded blue banner announced. It was a short ride on the 208 bus from the office he was working in that day which meant he could do a fairly decent session and, with a quick change, he could be back at his desk within about an hour and a quarter.

Ladywell Pool is a very old pool. So old they call it 'baths' rather than 'pools'. The website stated it was a 33 meter pool but Keith suspected in the old days it would have been referred to as a 36 2/3 yard pool. This made it difficult to practice the holy grail of the 50 meter dash, if there were to be a dad's race.

There were two tri-athletes who asked Keith for stroke technique advice and an over sixties lady who wanted to learn how to do tumble turns. Keith duly helped them at the expense of his own session.

Keith was beginning to get the power back and his muscles were beginning to tone up. He was covering more yardage in the session and his speed had increased. Keith reduced to 1 minute and 10 seconds on the last 100 meters of his judgement set. Things were looking bright.

Four months to go until his children would be competing in the club champs and he, perhaps the dads' race. Keith was practicing his sprinting. He even risked embarrassment in the public sessions by practicing his dives.

He thought through his race and tried out variations on breathing patterns and stroke rates to see which one was fastest. He thought about what part of the race he would look to see where the other dad competition was.

Thursday about 2.30pm. Thinking back to his heavy training days and basking in the glow of the lunchtime session, Keith thought it would be a marvellous idea to buy some dry land stretch resistance cords so he could build up muscle strength in between his sessions in the pool.

Saturday morning. The purchase complete, Keith attached them to a nail in the fence in his garden. He cracked on.

This was easy. He was stronger than he thought! He pulled the elastic cords in the motion of his swim strokes.

He did some extra exercises with the cords for all-round fitness. A bit of stretching over the head, back round the body and even around to the side.

He pushed the rigorous workout with the cords to at least 25 minutes.

Keith couldn't move his arms the next day. Keith couldn't swim in the pool for a week and a half. Keith was an old fool.

Chapter 17

Ken

Nine straight days in the office in London and Keith finally managed to bag a day at home. Keith was busy tapping the keys on his computer to round another component part of the project off - he was never happier than when he was in control. Keith's attention was diverted for a moment by a movement in the shed. He could see Heggie through the now curtain lined windows of his shed and he studied him for several minutes.

Heggie was animated one minute and listening intently the next. Keith could only see the back of the other person. Keith squinted in the bright sunshine; it looked like an older man, a colossal man judging from the broadness of his shoulders.

From their positioning and their body language, it looked like more of a social, especially as Heggie was in the listening side of the shed. Keith wondered what the aging rock man would have in common with, what looked like a pensioner. Given the hilarity of Heggie's demeanour, Keith thought he would join them.

'Good afternoon,' Keith called out in advance as he approached the shed - he didn't want give anyone a heart attack. A new set of headlines formed in Keith's head:

'ELDERLY MAN DIES IN BIZARRE SHED GATHERING CULT' Elderly man dies in bizarre circumstances in shed gathering cult. Two local men (they always used 'local' in the Bucks Free

Press), thought to be in their 60s (how could they) *are in custody today....'*

Keith was pulled from his newspaper reporting by the sight of sign above the shed entrance which read

'Licensee. Hector A. Pump. Licensed to serve alcoholic beverages.'

'Come on in Keith,' cried Heggie, 'take no notice of that sign; I just put it up there to amuse Ken. You probably know Ken as he lives next door to you – and now all of the chiefs from the neighbouring lands have met, at this ceremonial site.'

Keith thought it was a nice way of putting something that actually meant the whole ruddy neighbourhood seemed to be hanging out in his shed.

Ken did indeed live next door to Keith, having moved there a number of years ago with his wife, Joyce, to be nearer their son and daughter in law. Ken was a large man, and he was still enormous despite being in his late 80s. His wife was small in comparison, with deep blue comforting eyes and a nice line in 'Littlecroft' marmalade, named after their bungalow. Joyce had a wonderful view on life and never seemed to worry about a thing. Keith's children always gave her an unconditionally large hug whenever they saw her, for no reason other than she was Joyce. There was a fairly regular exchange of flapjacks from Ford and Carina and marmalade the other way.

Joyce was 83 years old, but could still put on a family meal for 20 with little fuss. Keith always imagined them in their early years in Yorkshire –

Ken having stridden at least 10 miles across the dales with two sides of sheep and a bag of coal strapped to his back on a Friday night. The sheep would be quickly processed by Joyce and the fire would be stoked. Ken would then produce a small gift for her out of one of the folds of his enormous and heavy overcoat and she would smile one of her gentle smiles, peck him on the cheek and say, 'thank you dear'.

'I like what you have done with the shed,' Ken said 'very des res!' Ken talked loudly as his hearing was poor, but he was clearly tickled by the comfies such as the curtains, lamp and hat stand.

'You two know each other then?' enquired Keith, wishing to know more about the unlikely alliance.

'Yes,' replied Ken, 'came though my hedge he did, one Thursday, comes most Thursday afternoons in the summer.'

'Why Thursdays?'

'Gardening programme on my wireless,' replied Ken 'it was the shrubs and soft fruit special which lured him over, amazing what you can learn on the wireless.'

'You should see his runner beans!' chipped in Heggie, 'and Mrs Wardle always includes me in a drop of whiskey!' chinking his glass with Ken's. They were both chuckling like school children high on a feast of fizzy worms and sour cola bottles.

It was extremely evident that Heggie was interested in Ken. In fact, Heggie seemed to be interested in everything. 'Interested' was the first of three words that Keith would use if he had to describe Heggie. He was interested in things that you wouldn't ever think this rocked out guy would be. Gardeners' Question Time, runner beans, all people.

There was music playing.   Before Keith could ask - Heggie grandly announced 'the change in the format today is due to all music pre 1959 being 'sharing music', so rule number 2 don't apply.   With 1950's and before music, one would share the experience, they knew how to socially interact - it's the way they did it.   Ken has been telling me about his life and the act of him being born started World War 1 you know,' and they both erupted in laughter and chinked their glasses again.

'What's that lovely smell?' Keith asked.

'You're in for a bit of a treat,' Heggie replied. 'Welcome to one of our potato tasting sessions! One of the radio programmes we listened to last year was all about the humble potato, or rather the grand potato depending on your outlook.   Since that programme, Ken and I have been growing our own potatoes - and we have tasting sessions.'

'He's rigged up a heating thingy to keep them warm.   Heating dolly,' Ken said, gesturing admiringly at the unit stood in the corner.

'Just a hostess trolley shell really, with a modification of hot bricks to overcome the lack of electricity.   Here we have some nutty new potatoes from my garden, cooked about an hour ago, slicked with some best British butter and some chopped chives from my herb garden,' Heggie said, handing Keith a small ramekin of potatoes and a fork. 'Scientists have just finished sequencing the genome of the potato. I bet you didn't know that the potato has 39,000 genes, that's twice as many as Ken here, well not just Ken, all of us.

'And if that is not enough,' Ken added 'the flower of the potato plant is as beautiful as any rose you care to produce.'

'Here's a ramekin of Ken's fat and thrice-cooked-in-dripping chips, it's a winner!'

'These really are delicious!' Keith said chomping on a piping hot chip.

'Glass of whiskey with some ice?' Heggie enquired, opening a small fridge packed with ice blocks to keep a tray of smaller cubes cold, 'or there is some German Riesling which goes very well with the potato. I say German as you can get Riesling from anywhere now can't you Ken, how times have changed 'eh!'

'Only from Germany when I was your age,' Ken confirmed.

'The Riesling would be wonderful.'

'Last week, Ken's creamy dauphinoises triumphed over my silky pommes purees and the gnarled leathery jacket potatoes that I had rubbed with my secret ingredient and baked in the oven for six hours. Next week if you are around, we have Ken's boulangeres going spud to spud with my crunchy goose fat roasties. At the end of it all we will have a final and an overall winner!'

And there it was - scenes of generations mixing and sharing, at comfort with each other. Heggie surprised Keith on many occasions, the interest he had in people, the respect he showed and that day, the intensity of the relationship he had developed with Ken.

.oOo.

This is Keith's mind. I quite envy Ken in some respects, now retired and mooching around listening to gardening programmes. I could do that. I wouldn't have to work too hard and suffer the trials of everyday life. Having said that though, it can be a fine line between engaging and not engaging - and then not engaging with society and the society not engaging with you. The fear is that you can't pull back and stop the inertia and you start to drift. Apart from the blood clot that is lodged in the auxiliary vessel in the right thigh, the broken ribs and the swelling, we were doing okay generally in life.

All this laying around has got me thinking, which, I agree, is my primary function. We're on the edge you know. Everything is generally good - but there are just some things you can't control. As I said, I've been thinking. We were doing quite well up until this rather unfortunate 'accident'. I've been enjoying sorting and logging all the images and thoughts nicely into their categories – I'm quite good at that. I'm also pretty good at taking the bad stuff and isolating it pretty quickly so Keith doesn't have to think about it too much. The Ken story is one of my favourites, I retrieve it every now and again when I think it will do Keith some good.

Quite a lot of this stuff I've stopped is actually pretty scary. Keith has lost his Gramps six months ago and this was a new experience. The thoughts about Gramps are filed away but I can't seem to cover them or hide them behind other files. They are raw and burn with the intensity of ignited magnesium, shining in my thought vault, lighting everything around them. Talk about running at 150% on the emotions and on the thought process – never before witnessed and the power has been incredible. Gets you thinking that does.

I wonder what Gramp's mind was thinking. Us minds you know used to be able to communicate to a certain extent, Keith read about it once in a book, but we have lost that ability now. I'm guessing here - but we would like to know, as this is going to happen to us sometime. I won't *have much to do if it happens when Keith's in this state, I suppose I'll just flicker out, none of the senses with me.*

I know Gramps wanted to go quickly and without pain, 'slip away when asleep' as he told Keith. That didn't happen, although it was fairly peaceful in the end.

We just can't get away from this sadness, it's been six months and, although inevitable, it's still unjust somehow. Where can Keith's love for his Gramps go now? We can't redirect it, we have enough for everyone else and this is Gramp's love. Perhaps that's it; we just can't connect this love to anything tangible and we are lost. We were very fortunate though to have known him and meant something to him.

I expect his mind was terrified, like I would be. His mind was working well but the messages weren't getting through to the legs and that. He was sending messages but not getting anything back. The lungs were filling with fluid and the heart wasn't working well enough to get it away. We're a finely tuned machine you know, balanced but with a number of interdependencies.

It must have been like he was walking out on a downward sloping outcrop of rock, a peninsular. The ground beneath him was getting thinner and more precarious, he would have known it. The ground was crumbling from the underside, falling in bits to the void below. He just couldn't get back up the slope to the firm ground, he wanted to - but it was never going to be possible. There was no way back so he kept edging on; walking alongside with time, closer and closer to the more unstable ground.

Chapter 18

Times, They are a Changing

It was Saturday afternoon and Keith was cutting the grass before preparing a barbeque. His ideal would be to cut nice lines however, his lawnmower just didn't cut it and the plethora of multi coloured plastic toys scattered around made it difficult in any case.

Heggie appeared.

'On your own?' enquired Keith, looking behind Heggie to see if anyone else was coming through the hedge.

'Yeah, the current Mrs Pump has gone shopping and Daphne has gone home – I thought I would just say 'hi'. I reckoned I could hear the unmistakable sound of a Flymo roller rotary Ventura Turbo 350. I've got one of those for my lawn at the front – doesn't give you lines though so I've had to rig up a weighting system and set it on the cock.'

'You seem a bit down,' Keith said, noticing the tone of Heggie's voice.

'A bit.'

'Probably the lull after a busy week of house guests.'

'I think you could be right.' Heggie replied nodding in melancholy.

'Glass of the old vinos?' enquired Keith, thinking that any time is a good time for a small glass of red wine.

'Sounds very reasonable, the sun is above the yard arm,' replied Heggie looking up to the gable end of Keith's house as one would have done in the olden days, 'somewhere in the world.'

They sat together in the sunshine on the log from the tree Keith felled last year and was using a seat. They were both enjoying the wine on offer. The uncomplicated nature of the day was wonderful.

'I used to get a bit down after a swimming competition,' Keith offered, 'all the excitement and razzmatazz of competing. When you've trained nine times a week, competition was what it was all about. When you've expended copious amounts of energy and deployed vast quantities of adrenaline, there is only one way to go really – and that's down.'

'You should do it again Keith. It would be good for you to have a focus and get the old body nice and fit. I don't suppose you've felt anything recently quite like the adrenaline rush you did back then.'

'No, nothing's come close really. I've thought about it a lot, particularly now that Ford and Carina are swimming in the club and competing. The waft of chlorine as you approach the sports centre, the buzz of uber fit athletes applying their craft, the early mornings, the hard graft. The small waves of adrenaline as you think about your race. The gushing of adrenaline as you stand behind the blocks for your race. Legs slightly jelly. Yeah, I think I should do it. It might just save me from myself.'

'That's good then! Get the old budgie smugglers ready and go for it! Dust of the old banana hanger and get in there!'

They sat quietly for a time. Keith considered the return to the pool and made the commitment mentally. Heggie considered what he could do to rekindle any sort of adrenaline rush.

'I'm preparing some food for the barbeque. I'd like it if you could stay and eat with us.

97

Carina's seen you and backed me up by vouching for your existence, but she has quite a number of imaginary friends that the rest of the family don't think you exist. We often play a game on the way to my Mum's house as we pass those flats next to the retail park in Wycombe Marsh; it's called 'what's on the balcony today?' Usually it's the washing, a bike and a sandpit turned on its side but sometimes it can be a deflated paddling pool in the summer or cardboard boxes just after Christmas – no people though, not enough room. Carina now plays a game called 'who's in the shed today!'

'I tell my children such tall stories that they think you're my alter-ego. They don't believe the guests you've had in the shed. They also don't believe that my mother-in-law leads the band at the Wycombe Wanderer's football games by playing the great escape on her trumpet.'

Heggie chuckled. It was possible that Keith's family was questioning if he did exist.

'You say the current Mrs Pump is out shopping - been married before?' asked Keith sucking the top layer off of his glass of wine and drawing in air to enhance the flavour of his Sainsbury's house red 3L boxed wine.

Heggie took his empty glass from the table and drained another from the box. 'Never been married before but I have two wives, well two lovers who come and look after me – on a kinda rotation basis. I'm not sure how they sort it out really, but one of them is always around. Monica and Nophelia.

The children came through the opened patio doors into the garden like two cannonballs.

'It's going to be a story for another time Keith,' and Heggie turned and introduced himself to Ford and Carina.

'They've really cheered me up Keith, I'm delighted they laughed at my stories and I'm entertained that they had to keep asking you and your good lady if they were true. Ah, I'm as happy as a Rioja wine maker. Isn't it great Keith, if you are a wine maker you can think to yourself that somewhere in the world you are bringing happiness to someone.'

'I suppose that it is a bit like being a musician, Heggie. People are listening to your creation at some point, somewhere in the world. I've heard people refer to pieces of music as their 'life raft' on occasions it means that much to them. Powerful stuff.'

The children were going out to see their grandparents, to have Chinese takeaway and watch the early evening dancing show on TV. Heggie and Keith agreed to meet up in the shed in 10 minutes. This would allow Keith time to tidy away the remaining things and lock up the front of the house.

Keith collected the recently emptied bottle under the duster pile from the sink cupboard. He went outside and picked up the half sized gin bottle from behind the log store next to the front door. Keith rummaged them down into the glass recycling bin, under last week's bottles. It could be difficult secreting the physical evidence when Keith had 'taken off' again. Keith rationalised that cutting down the intake meant not producing so many empty wine bottles; it didn't include finishing the remnants of spirit bottles – that was just good housekeeping.

Keith checked the close for activity. No-one was around. He took the 10 pack of Marlborough Lights from his pocket and lit up behind the trees. When he was a student, he used to call packs of

10 a 'poverty pack'. Now they were useful as they were easily concealed in the pocket or his work bag. The wind was blowing in the right direction and disappeared through next door's hedge and not in the direction of the shed. He hid the butt right next to the trunk of a tree, under some holly leaves, popped in some strong chewing gum, took off his smoking glove, gave his hands a squirt of hand gel just to be sure, and headed off in the direction of the shed.

The starlings were chattering in the trees. A cat was curling itself up on a neighbour's shed roof. Keith was tipsy and the sun was shining. He was euphoric with his life.

Heggie was just squeezing the inner silver lining of the wine box into a glass when he arrived.

'So what is it you love so much about the fags Keith?'

Keith was taken aback.

'It's my well-kept secret,' he stammered.

'What? With great plumes of smoke rising up through the hedge, the constant chewing on menthol gum and the heavy wear to your front tooth, the nagging cough and the slight whiff of antibacterial solution emanating from your hands - it's hardly a well-kept secret!'

Keith knew the game was well and truly up with Heggie. He thought for a moment and opened up.

'I suppose I love the packaging, the hit, the freedom to walk into any shop and purchase, the choice - just don't tell the wife.'

'Surely it's a case of love me, love my fags?'

'It's idiotic is what it is. Two young children, constant coughs and colds, the dancing bears in your head telling you that it is time for another, the short temper and the feeling of failure, that's what it is. Plus it's costing me a fair bit of money to be this unwell. I have a profound and constant sadness, a sort of grieving over what I'm doing – but I just keep doing it.'

'Can you imagine the sadness you are going to cause Keith? I'm not even going to ask you what it is about the booze, I get the picture. Here's your glass of wine, me old addict.'

'I'll do the swimming thing,' Keith thought. *'That will be my driver.'*

Heggie continued. 'I've been thinking about this a lot Keith, I drink and smoke because I'm selfish, I enjoy it and I've got nothing else to do. What's really with you?'

Both quite squiffy, they sat there pondering.

'Cheese,' Heggie suddenly announced. It was a dramatic way in which to change the subject. 'He was a magazma man of the finest quality. Hung round with Led Zep a lot you know.'

'This sounds like it's going to be a good one, I'll go back to the house and source us some more wine,' Keith suggested.

'Never fear,' Heggie shouted rather too loudly, 'I've an emergency bottle in each shed, I'll be one secondo.'

Keith, you are feeling very squiffy and you know at this point you should lay off. It's okay for you, you can just carry on, it's me that has to keep everything going you know when you nod off or fall over. Don't think you are cloaked in the full invincibility armour and can just do what you want.

Heggie was back.

'Quick release,' he said, twisting the screw cap on the bottle of red. 'I'm finished with corks; screw caps are the way forward. I've brought some diet coke if you prefer something softer?'

Take the diet coke, don't just plough on with the wine! You know you've reached that point at which you are about to take off and it will all go horribly wrong!

'I'll plough on with the wine thanks Heggie, although I think I've reached that point where it could all go horribly wrong. I've just got to push through it.'

Doh! Wrong answer!

'Why did they call him Cheese?' Keith enquired, his eyes starting to point in different directions.

'Because that's his name, Hubert Cheese. I was having a nice pint of ale last Tuesday with Hubert Cheese and Robert Plant, you know, the lead singer from Led Zeppelin. We were in 'The Mitre' pub, that's a priest's hat to you Keith, in Stourbridge. It was very busy for a Tuesday night and we were keeping ourselves to ourselves, mainly for Robert's sake. The clientele were predominantly young thrusters with long, black, polished hair, tied back into pony tails or left free to flow to enable the flick or the pull behind the ears. Then a funny thing happened Keith. Have a guess Keith what happened to have pertained that evening.'

'Don't tell me, you were all barred for being too boisterous! The shame of it, but I didn't read anything in the papers.'

'No.'

'Mr. Plant won the jackpot on the fruit machine and was so surprised that he choked on a peanut – I quite like the idea of a rock legend playing a tuppney nudger.'

102

'Wrong again. You'll never guess so I'll tell you. In the space of 60 seconds, I was moved from where I was sitting enjoying my ale in my pint jug with a handle, into the old boy envelope, not physically you understand, but metaphorically and emotionally speaking. There were a few references being made to Led Zep being a rubbish band. It was only banter and all that, but a bit rich when it's being directed at a man who has sold kazillion billion million records worldwide with Led Zep and even more as a solo artist and other collaborations and having sustained a career over at least 190 years.

'Then someone shouted out "Planty, Planty, his head's in the crap." I was puzzled by this one I had to admit. I couldn't understand for one minute why young Mr Plant's head would have anything to do with being stuck in crap, I always considered him to be grounded and a well thought out kinda chap. Thank goodness Hubert was on hand to translate the intensely Brummie accent - that the offender was actually saying "Planty, Planty, Zeppelin are crap".

'I realised that although quite good humour, the gulf of respect had opened up. The amazing career didn't account for 'owt on the face of it. I started to have a think about my legacy and achievement and how it was seen by others. It's a painful area you know when you start to get to my age. Well, we went back to our cribbage and nothing more was said however, the grey cloud these thoughts created still hovers on my erstwhile sunny horizon. Planty won six games to my four.

'Hubert found it difficult to settle when Led Zep split. He lived on the roof of my turret the whole summer, only coming down to the outside toilet and for a bath in the pond once a week. We used to invite him for his Sunday lunch and he would arrive at the front door at 12.30pm prompt for drinks and nibbles, bizarrely, dressed in a white tuxedo. At about 3.30pm, having finished his cheese and crackers and polished off a port, he would rise and declare he had better make tracks and left back through the front door before returning to the turret.

'The rest of the time, I had to send up food in a basket. I would have to shout up to him the basket was ready. He was a bit deaf so I had to make sure my shouts were 'gouder'. Forget it Keith if you don't get it, it's a cheese related joke. He said his goodbyes one day, had a final blast in the pond and disappeared. He lived in Switzerland for quite some time as a reclusive 'casooner', that's a goat herder to you Keith. He was slowly detaching from conventional society by 'dropping out'. He was doing nothing - which is the purest form of drugs, the opiate of the mad and the lazy. More recently, he has been feeding the conveyor belt of young bands elevation to potential stardom. It's hard graft trolling around those clubs and pubs, pretty unrewarding and not very lucrative.'

Heggie was leaning forward, holding his head in his hands and shaking his head. 'I just couldn't see the point of him working so hard, but he's the one who's got the purpose, he's the one with the direction, not me.'

There was an uncomfortable pause whilst Heggie did some more head shaking. Keith felt it could have gone either way. Heggie pulled his head up from his hands and poured both of them a top up.

'Less of my worries Keith, lighten the mood and entertain us by telling me just what it is that you do.'

Somewhat relieved at the pause in proceedings, an escape if you like, Keith took a hefty slug of his drink and illuminated Heggie on the wonders of his working life.

'I've been working contracts, interim, projects and the like. I was made redundant three years ago from what seemed a secure job. The business I was working for had merged and the other chief executive had taken the top job. There ensued a picking off of my fellow managers by the other management team which is fairly standard stuff. I took redundancy rather that the different position which had been offered.

'I'd rather do something else you know. I'd like to be out of that rubbish, playing the corporate game. I'd like to write. I feel alive when I write. I'd like to be like the David Bowie of the writing world. He set his stall out – it was on his terms. He created some masterpieces – the life raft of many a person for sure. He constructed lyrics that he wanted to – created and recreated himself, did what he wanted. I'd like to sit in the garden on a sunny day and be the writing David Bowie – out of the wind and hot in the sun.'

'Ooh, I might be able to help you there – sitting in the sun out of the wind rather than being the DB of the writing world. The latter is rather for you to do but I've an invention to help you with the former,' Heggie enthused.

'That sounds great! Anyway, you asked me what it is I do, not what I would like to do. For my current career, I have to travel. Not the exciting, exotic travel but the more mundane, tedious travel to and from various locations in London and the Home Counties, mainly in and around London though,' Keith continued.

'Mostly I walk to the bus stop to get the bus down the hill to the station. The bus comes at

6:49am or rather it doesn't. Depending on the driver it can come either five minutes before the scheduled time or ten after. When the mad man with the facial piercings is driving, it's ahead of schedule. Then, the bus hurtles down the hill at breakneck speed, the passengers holding on for dear life, only to spin round the terminus turning circle at the train station, sending commuters for cover and missing cars by only inches. It will then sit there for 10 minutes as it's early. Sometimes I cycle to the station. I have to dodge the potholes as well as the crazy bus driver who is ahead of schedule and sits about two foot from the back of my rear wheel!'

Heggie leaned back in the recliner and raised his glass in encouragement for the story to continue.

'When I started to work in London, my journey was chaotic, different trains and different routes but I soon settled into a routine. I became part of the 7:01am club who catch the train from Great Missenden to Marylebone. I'm part of a smaller band who walk down to Baker Street tube station to catch the Jubilee Line, an even smaller band who reached Southwark and the only one who then heads for platform A at Waterloo East for a wee break before joining a new group of two who catch the 8:16am from platform B to Catford Bridge. I tend to avoid the larger connecting stations such as London Bridge and Charing Cross with their multiple platforms and busy concourses. It's too mad with people darting in all directions. Marylebone is rather genteel compared to its bigger brothers, or sisters. I can't remember what gender stations are.

'I've mentioned this before to you Heggie. There are always the same faces. The guy with a grey, waxed moustache, standing next to the shoe shine, shimming from one foot to the other every three seconds and then a circular walk every other minute. The group of five that wait at Amersham to get on the train. The tall chap of the group always peers in through the window and notifies the rest of the group if there are seats together, but what he is really saying is "the rest of you on this station – just don't try it." Comical.

'The same people go through the barriers on the return journey and wait on the platforms to get a steal on their fellow passengers and then would say things like "it usually goes from platform two you know" when platform six is called and they find themselves at the back of the queue. The same people will run past the old and the families in order to get the best seat, the cads. I always boo them.'

Heggie continued to listen from the recliner in a fine stupor.

'The seasons come and go, signified by the dress code. Shirts in the summer for the chaps, shirts and suits as we approach the autumn and then overcoats. With the ladies it manifests itself in a crescendo of sandals, shoes and then boots and then back again. I watch people too much and making eye contact with people is not a good thing, especially in some parts of London. I got shouted out regularly by the youths in Stevenage "hey Mr. Pin stripes, hey fancy shoes". In Brixton I was asked to help with financial contributions and donations of tobacco. I soon learnt that you should carry an empty packet of cigarettes so you could gesture - oh, I would have given you one but their all gone. By the time I was working in Lewisham, I kept my head down and learnt that you should carry a second wallet. At least forty people get a knife pulled on them every day in London. I think you are more likely to get targeted if you are a male as mugging old people and women seems more heinous to the Police and the courts. It seems more okay to mug younger and dare I say it middle aged men.

"Pod' friendships are formed on the basis of preference of carriage. The 'pods' would know where the train doors would arrive so they huddle together. They collectively groan when there is a short service in appreciation that some of their 'pod' members wouldn't make it into a seat and would have to stand. At least the 7.01 was the fast service to Marylebone and it shaves a cool 3 minutes off the journey time of 48 minutes.

'I always like to see the train coming around the corner and feel like cheering, but I never do. On the return journey I feel like letting out a whoop when the driver calls out 'Greeeeaaaat Missenden' but again, I never do. Great Missenden Station is my favourite. Not just because it is my 'hometown' station but it has class. The red and blue painted ornate iron columns are rather in-keeping with the grand Marylebone Station. The paving is detailed where other stations just have municipal flag stones. The roof has character with a white cut wood facia and even the chain link fencing comes in red. The staff still take the trouble to do hanging baskets in the summer and make up little presentation themed scenes on the counter – whether it be Wimbledon, Christmas shopping or a Royal type event.

'The stairs on the round covered walkway are uneven and irregular and I thank the Lord that the people who make the decisions at Chiltern Railway decided a 'mind the irregular steps' sign would do rather than replacing this characteristic with a flight of standard concrete steps with plastic trims.'

Heggie grinned in contentment at the image of Little Britain still being alive and well in Great Missenden.

'This is the first station on the route coming out of London that doesn't have Oyster touch-ins or ticket barriers to go through. It seems like the last bastion of decency and honesty where travellers can be trusted to do the right thing. When they do check though, they always catch a few people every train who are ticket dodging. It was a fairly traumatic experience for most people when they replaced the old, fat, ceiling hung monitors with the flat screen, wall mounted neon LED screens last year. It was like someone was nudging the new world on this peaceful and essentially English station.

'I just love those people who run for trains but actually don't seem to move any faster than they would do walking, despite all the effort and in most cases the noise. I would love to bend over and shout encouragement as they do in the Tour de France – 'come on, go, go, go, pumpo, you can do it, allez allez allez! But I might get thumped. Cheery goodbyes are offered to fellow passengers at Marylebone as people disappeared onto the underground or through the arches onto the street. I sometimes feel I would like to gesture and wave, but I travel alone.

'There are however presents throughout my journey. Random meetings between people and the oversized 'ooh hellos' who aren't really that much friends, otherwise they would be in contact with each other all the time. There are minor stumbles on doors and escalators with the following split second decisions being taken to either ignore what had happened, to look round and be cross at the offending hazard or to be self deprecating and act like a fool. I play the 'rediculant' game of spotting daft things people carry on the underground. I've seen an oversized empty glass fish tank - complete with the diver's chest and plastic weed. I've seen trolleys of bedding plants being wheeled through dense crowds and five long strip lighting tubes taped together with selotape – how dangerous is that? The best though was a guy with a tent and three sleeping bags - but I can't give myself first prize.'

'I expect it can be fairly anonymous this travelling malarkey?' Heggie asked.

'It can be. I can quite often go a whole return journey and not speak to anyone. It's all very grinding. I feel a sense of responsibility somehow being a frequent user of the trains to make everything okay. There are lots of nationalities trying to find their way around, semi lost, particularly around the Edgware Road bit where there are two stations, called the same, but about 500 yards apart and with different lines going through them. I often wish to help but I'm not very good at the old lingo – I should really, being an 'elder' of the tubes now. I've only helped one American fella. On vacation he was, following the legends of British rock he told me. He had a gnarled look with part of his ear missing – expect he lost it in some booze fuelled caper with one of the big American rock bands. I recounted my story of Fish and the cans of beer and nearly being run over by a Bee-Gee in Gerrards Cross. I told him there were loads of them around the home counties – Deep Purple in Gerrards Cross, Iron Maiden in High Wycombe, Jethrow Tull in Flackwell Heath, Marillion in Aylesbury, Ozzy in Chalfont and of course you out Great Missenden way. He was quite impressed I think. Did my bit for tourism and international relations that day.

110

'Coffee seems to plays a large part in people's travel. It appears to me that a large section of the nation has become unable to operate without coffee and then, when they have a coffee, they can't operate properly. There is no easy solution to juggling bags and coffee without any natural resting points. I'm highly entertained by these coffee bearers who run for trains and buses. The rules for this seems to be that you:

Firstly have to have a napkin folded around the coffee cup to lessen your grip and make it more difficult to hold;

Secondly have to be in possession of an oversized bag or briefcase – usually hanging off the arm carrying the coffee; and

Finally, you have to move your legs in an unusual way and take mini steps in order to keep the coffee level.

'I think a new word is needed for this phenomenon and my offering to the English language is 'the sambachino', geddit – half coffee, half dance.'

'Bravo,' Heggie added, raising his glass and shifting his body position slightly more upright so he could access the bottle.

'Branded coffee cups are now the thing and I lament the days of the simple, plain polystyrene cups with no markings apart from the teeth marks sunk into them around the rim. Very satisfying biting into a polystyrene cup, a little like drawing on the smooth rubber sole of your slippers.

'Perilous this travel business though. It's easy to soak up the time with a quick drink. How easy it is to get into the habit. Twenty minutes till the train leaves – time for a swift half at the Station Inn at Marylebone. I'll catch the next one. I'm ashamed to say that I've waited for the long service train with numerous carriages so I can sit on my own and have a drink or two on board from a can or a mini bottle of wine from the Marks and Spencer or the cheap cartons of Spanish red from Tesco – easy to carry and secrete in your bag. I used to think drinking on a train was just for the sad, but I can see the point of it now and most of the time I go for it, irrespective of what other people might think, even when I'm in a really busy carriage and risk being seen by any of the dads from school. One can for such occasions or if I know I'm catching the 18.03 long service, then it's two cans as I'll almost definitely get a double seat to myself.

'It started with a can on a Friday night on the train on the way home as a treat and then progressed to a can each night. The treat on Friday night is now something a bit more special, a more expensive can of import or something similar or two cans. Inertia.'

Keith drew breath.

'I'm stood on a beach Heggie.'

Oh, here we go – no need to go there, the beach thing is something that should stay up here, between the two of us.

'The beach is steep. It runs down to the deep sea. The sand is soft. It's soft and moving under my feet as I tread forward.'

Heggie was now bold upright. His hand movement stopped and he held it outstretched for the bottle, listening intently as Keith continued.

Keith did continue, speaking quickly.

'I'm unsteady and my steps are slow. This drinking thing is starting to be a problem. I'm enjoying it and it's getting regular. It's not a problem but I'm not wholly sure I could stop or would want to stop if I needed to. I've said I would, just to spite those who say I've a problem. 'I gave up just because of you I'd say'. If I don't keep it in check I'll be in the sea, it would be a quick process I'm sure and there would be no paddling at first; it's up here on the sand or right in. I'll be straight up to my neck in this sea, out of my depth, controlled by the swell and the current, gone, but still there, bobbing, helpless, out of reach from everyone but still visible for those who love me or would wish to look for me. It's the people who love me that it would be most unjust for. You're not human if you are not loved. They love me unconditionally and I'm doing this!'

Heggie was out of his chair. He thumped his empty glass down and his eyes were wide open. His face was now just inches from Keith's as Keith continued.

'It's crazy, Heggie. I've got everything and no worries but I'm just messing it up with fags and booze, why?'

'I'm with you buddy, I'm with you. I'm on the beach with you.' Heggie grabbed the front of Keith's shirt with both hands and held onto them with tight fists. 'I've been in the sea, I'm back on the beach, but I'm heading for the sea again. I've got everything as well, two wives, an orchard, seven sheds and a pond you can have a bath in. I used to have a sense of direction Keith, a purpose, a plan if you like, I could see where I fitted in and where I was going. What happened to my childhood dreams?'

Heggie was rocking Keith back and forwards by his shirt. 'Hell, I had dreams, loads of them but I can't even remember them now. That Richards from the Stones told me that I should never forget my heroes – he was right, and I have. Looking at

113

it now it seems I have no focus. I'm doubting it all again Keith.'

Heggie loosened his grip, suddenly realising what he was doing and smoothed out Keith's shirt. With a large intake of air and a gulp of wine he concluded 'I think I've lost my way Keith, I might have to do a Hubert.'

They both sank back into their recliners.

I wasn't expecting that! From either of them! Maybe we should have some music to get us back to normal. How about it Keith?

After about 30 seconds, Keith suggested they had some music. 'Let's have a bit of Lynyrd Skynyrd's 'Coming Home' to perk us up a bit.'

Chapter 19

Bag Lady

Keith roused to the vibrant track of Lynyrd Skynyrd's 'You run around'. It was the last track on the album and always seemed to be a bit louder than the rest. It was the track that often woke Keith up. He was groggy. Waking after booze was no fun. Keith looked around. Heggie was gone.

Keith located the portal in the hedge and he took the opportunity to go through into Heggie's garden. Although they were getting on like old pals, Keith didn't really know Heggie that well - apart from sharing some common ground on the beach. He didn't know what Heggie would do next. The bit about 'doing a Hubert' worried him somewhat.

The end of the garden was well tended for an end of a garden. Everything seemed to be natural but planned and well ordered. There were no dead-heads and no failings in the edges to the grassed areas. Keith spotted Heggie's feet protruding from one of the herbaceous borders. Keith approached. He looked dead, but only dead drunk hopefully.

'Heggie,' Keith called out. He could see the headline now:

'TRAGIC DEATH AMONG THE GLADIOLI. Mysterious local man found dead in his flowers, no note left and the Police are treating it as suspicious. Cocktail of booze and Lynyrd Skynyrd surrounds this mystery. Neighbour, a man in his late 50's who saw him last is being held.'

Keith moved closer.

'Heggie?' he called quietly.

There was no movement. Keith couldn't detect any rise or fall in Heggie's chest from where he was standing. 'Holy shit. I'm going to have to touch him to see if he is still warm. I'm right in the frame here. I hope they can establish it was natural causes or something.' The quietness of the garden personified the seriousness of the situation. Keith leaned over. He was close enough to see the fine wrinkles around Heggie's eyes. There was nothing. Not even a twitch. Keith reached out his hand towards Heggie's face. The back of his fingers were about a centimetre away from his cheek. Would he be stone cold?'

'Ah-ha Keith, welcome to my garden!' Heggie shouted buoyantly as he jumped up with a flick like a break-dancer. It was an impressive move under any circumstances but not appreciated by Keith at this particular moment. Keith leapt back holding his chest and shook to his core. 'Did you enjoy your snoozy-poos? I love the view from there – one of my favourite laying points, I have five dotted around the garden depending on my mood.'

'I'm pleased to see you so well you git, you scared the crap out of me,' said Heggie. 'I thought I had poisoned you with my barbeque cooking or you had done something silly.'

'Something silly? Not me you old fool, what would either Mrs Pump do without me to fuss about and me to cause them untold mischief!' Heggie demonstrated he was fighting fit by pretending to be a boxer – sparring with an imaginary opponent. 'Keith,' he declared after his display of moves had finished. 'I'd like to give this horse racing thing a go, come on into my shed for a cuppa and you can tell me all about it.'

116

Heggie strode across the immaculate lawn between the well turned out borders. Keith followed. He hadn't been made to jump like that in a while, since Heggie grabbed his foot in the shed in fact, and it took him a few minutes to calm down.

'We're heading to that one,' cried Heggie marching intently and pointing to a large workshop style shed in the far corner and past a series of other sheds. 'That's my favourite one, chaps only.' They marched on, the garden was substantial.

'The old one is a good one,' continued Heggie, setting a demanding pace and pointing to a small and quaint looking shed with a thatched roof with white Georgian looking panel windows. It's north facing so that is where I do my writing. Roald Dahl liked a north facing shed; it gives the right kind of light for writing. I do my answers for Gardeners Question Time in that shed and set questions for specialist sections of Mastermind and 'Are you smarter than a ten year old' – your children have probably watched that show Keith.'

'They have, on numerous occasions. I thought the questions were rather hard. Dick and Dom present.'

'They have a great future Dick and Dom. I've spent some time with them in that very shed planning how they will make the leap to mainstream. Once they do that, they could be as big as Ant and Dec you know, if they stop shouting 'bogies' in the street and sticking things on people. This is the gardener's shed, not that I have a gardener, so it's my shed when I'm the gardener if you like. I do all my cuttings and grow seedlings and the sort in there. That's also where I keep my Toulan Pro303 –that's a lawn mower to you Keith. It has a 54-inch cutting capability and a 2.6 HP Briggs and Stratton V-Twin engine. The special

117

feature is a hydrostatic foot pedal control, plus it has automatic transmission and cruise control. This particular lawn tractor handles well and will perform on hilly as well large parcels of land. It was the reference to 'lawn tractor' and 'parcel's' of land that got me Keith. The four-wheel steering is extremely maneuverable. The side dischargers mulch the clippings a further 30% or so on other models, which is better for the lawn – it's a beast and gives me an enormous sense of wellbeing.'

'Impressive.'

'The new shed is where I keep my music stuff,' Heggie said, pointing to a well-constructed shed of wooden ship-lapped frontage design. 'I record things these days, mainly for therapy purposes. I've been developing a system to help traumatised patients with their recovery. I told you about the racehorse, but the strangest thing I've ever done was to help some shy pandas mate at London zoo, through the use of a rousing melody. There is of course more to it than that, but you get the picture.'

Heggie slid the door sideways on the 'chap's only' shed. Keith was impressed. He had never seen a shed with such a large sliding door before.

'This must have been built for an old car I think,' explained Heggie. 'Don't be put off by all the jars and bottles.'

Along one side of the shed there were various jars, bottles and plastic containers. Some were full of different coloured liquids and others with an assortment of dry objects. There must have been hundreds of containers, all shapes and sizes. The shed was well ordered, clean with good quality shelving. It looked like a cross between a well ordered chemist and a mad scientist's lab. Keith peered closer at the ensemble of jars nearest to him. He couldn't make out what was in them at first. Grimly, he realised. *'Body parts!'* There were bits of hair, blood stained song sheets and small bits of human flesh. *'Goodness knows what the liquids are,'* he thought to himself. He subtly checked where Heggie was at that moment and was pleased to find he had a clear exit through the sliding door should he need to do so. Heggie had not assumed a confrontational or blocking body position.

'Am I safe in here with you Heggie? I'm not going to end up in one of these jars am I?'

'It's all Hardy Woodpecker's fault you know. I was backstage at a festival with a very problematic lead singer of a band on a meteoric rise to fame. When fame and glory hits a young band with a predetermined mindset for chaos and excess, all sorts of things can go wrong. Their management team had asked me to go on the road with them, as sort of a calming father figure. I always feel it is best to lead from the front on occasions such as these, so we got up to some high jinks I can tell you, but I always managed to get them on stage in the right city at about the right time.

'Woodpecker, the lead singer was a lunatic with a liking for velvet. Despite doing daft things like walking right along the light scaffolding high up above the stage - under the influence of alcohol, he suffered terrible pre-gig nerves. He would have to drink himself into a calmed state. One night, just before he was due to go on stage, he peed into one of those rather large slow release water containers you find stuck in pots of a weeping fig tree. He was desperate from the drink. Pleased with the amount he had done, he held it aloft for the other band members to admire.

As you can imagine Keith, liquid and electric guitars don't mix so I confiscated it before the inevitable happened and the bass guitarist ended up getting electrocuted. I held it aloft against the glaring lights of the stage - 'This is of good enough quality that I am going to sell it!' I told them.

'Alan 'Headbanger' Harris, the drummer of the 'Flaming Icicle Popsicles', that night's support band, staggered from the shadows at that point with a whiskey bottle in his hand. He pushed the warm offering into my hand and said 'you can sell that one as well if you like!' He then staggered off, shouting loudly to all that would hear him 'that Heggie Pump dude is selling pee you know – he's starting a new business selling rock pee!'

'It obviously tickled him greatly 'cos he seems to have told loads of people. That was twenty years ago and I still get jars of pee and various other stuff through the post – even today! Look, here is the end of a finger from Terrance Trantrum, bass guitarist with Terrance and the Tantrumettes, a clump of singed hair from that Pepsi advert and a piece of someone's ear left over from the stage at Montreal - donor unknown.

'I saw Hardy Woodpecker some ten years later on the set of Oliver Stone's 'The Doors' movie. He was telling Val Kilmer who was playing Jim Morrison about this story and they both found it hilarious - so I'm now getting stuff from the film world! I have a piece of Val Kilmer's skin here somewhere he sent me after an accident on the set of 'Heat'; he thought he would get in on the action as well! I still have a turnover of around £50,000 dealing with traders in this stuff. Don't even have to advertise, not that I would want to!'

Heggie showed Keith to the comfy area. It was more like a small kitchenette with a couple of two-seater sofas arranged around a small mirrored coffee table. He pulled up a fridge unit on wheels. The glass door showed an assortment of soft drink cans, bottled water and beers. Heggie switched on the coffee machine and placed an assortment of coffee pods on the table for Keith to choose at will.

'Now tell me Keith all about this horse racing stuff, I'm particularly interested in how it all started for you with the horses. I've got as far as researching that we have two bookmakers near here, one in the village and one in Great Missenden. Which one should I use?'

'I think it's a good idea for you to use a bookies Heggie. I have an online account, but going to the bookies will be good for you. There are people you'll meet at the bookmakers who have limited money and could usefully do with a new pair of trousers or a pair of shoes, usually both, but instead of getting them updated, they'll spend their money on each and every one of the afternoon races. Don't use the one in Great Missenden, those dodgy Robinson brothers have just taken it over and it has got a bad feel to it. You'll meet some interesting people racing Heggie, both at the bookies and especially at the racetrack. It is society polarised; your 'have's' and 'have not's'. Please promise me though Heggie, do keep it small and keep it fun otherwise it will ruin you.'

'Of course I will, I just want to…. what's the expression, bash the bookies and eke out a bit of value.'

'I started going to the racing with my old swim coach, Ralph when I was about 15 years old. It really is a different affair going to the races than going to a bookies. I recommend you get yourself dressed up and take both Mrs Pumps one day, have a picnic in the car park and a bit of bubbly before the racing and study form.

'Ralph teamed up with a guy called Ronnie and they bought a pitch at the track so they could be 'rails' bookmakers. Rails bookmakers take bets from other bookmakers who want to offset their potential liabilities on a particular horse as well as taking bets from punters. They're situated along the fence rails which separate the members and public areas of the racecourse – hence they call them 'rails' bookmakers. Ralph did a lot of work on which horses wouldn't win and Ronnie would offer slightly higher odds on those and they would try and make a profit by taking bets from the other bookmakers. This was fascinating stuff to me – I thought people looked for winners not losers! Ralph always said that the punter had one horse running for him and the rest of the field was running for the bookmaker. It was enough for me just going to the races, but this added element just put the icing on the cake.

'My Gramps was also always interested in horseracing and that rubbed off on me. He used to watch the racing on a Saturday afternoon. When I was a tiddler, it held no particular interest - but, I could see that it excited him! When I went to the races, I used to phone him at home for his selection and then shop around the bookmakers trackside to get him the best odds. My plan was to win big Heggie and buy a horse and call him Mr.T after Gramps. His surname was Tilling and we called him Mr. T, as well as the 'wise one' and the 'old bandit' after he had had a win. I would have taken the horse and Gramps to all the different tracks and we would have sent him jumping – the horse that is.'

'Like Desert Orchid?' Heggie interjected.

'Exactly right, what a horse Desert Orchid was! Now, Ralph knew which horses he thought couldn't win and he also knew the horses he felt had a good chance of winning - so Ronnie wouldn't accept bets from the other bookmakers on these. Ralph studied the time form, speed form, stable form, form, form, form! Did you know you can actually pay for information on which horses hadn't travelled well or which stables had a cough going around? That's a different type of tipping service – information is key. Other bookies would ask to lay off money with Ronnie if they had taken too much on one particular horse and you got to know which of the punters would win more often than not. Tying all this information up gave me a bit of an 'in' to which horses might win. What great fun! Now, having identified my list of potential winners, I would select the two which had the best chance and I would pop up to the Tote and have a small bet on the two to come first and second - in either order. I had only a little success but the payout was a real bumper if it worked.

'Ralph then teamed up with another bookmaker called Gary and this was the premier league. They weren't just laying a few horses now, they were taking bets from punters, big bets. They were 'boards' bookmakers as they put their prices up on those large boards. Be warned Heggie, you can get doomed at this game. I was with Ralph and Gary the day Frankie rode his seven winners. Gary lost a fortune on the last of the seven horses, Fujiama Crest. Gary had to sell his house and cars and was selling Christmas wrapping paper in Oxford Street to scrape the money to go racing in the afternoons. Gary still holds the record for taking the biggest bet ever placed on a greyhound track in this country – he lost.

'I also went with them one year to the Cheltenham Festival, the highlight of the jumping calendar. They lost more than my mortgage on the first race when the jolly, that's the favourite to you Heggie, Paddy's Return won. I simply couldn't bear to think about losing that level of wonga. They ended up about £8,000 on the day which I thought was a magnificent result, but traditionally; the Cheltenham Festival is where bookies can make enough to pay the private school fees for their children for the year.

'I used to help Ralph and Gary out by looking after the bag, sorting out the notes into hundreds and then thousands between races, taking the punters money and paying them out afterwards. Big bundles of the filthy lucre. They used to call me the 'Bag Lady'. I once saw them make a book where they couldn't lose, whatever the result, by carefully balancing bets on each horse and taking bets at one price and laying them off to other bookies at another price – what a great position to be in!

'I progressed to relaying prices to Ralph and Gary from the other boards when there was a market move, they even kitted me with a two way radio! My career however, was cut short one afternoon at a race meeting in Huntingdon, not that I was being paid or anything! Gary had asked me to go and lay a bet on with another bookmaker of '100 to 1300'. 'Easy' I thought so I went up to the first bookmaker and said 'please could I have 100 to 1300 for Gary.' He said 'you can have 13 to 169,' but I didn't have a clue what he was talking about. No other bookmaker would take my bet as Gary was seen as knowledgeable. Those buggers wiped the price of that particular horse off the board as I walked along the line. I headed back to Gary pretty pronto. The race had started

124

and thankfully they didn't lose but looking back at it now, I had rather left them exposed to losing £1,131. I hadn't twigged that I was betting £100 to win £1300. I think it was fairly justified they changed my name from 'Bag Lady' to 'Keith of Huntingdon'. They never let me lay off bets again.'

'Lucky escape for you,' Heggie said, taking it all in.

'If you're going to take up this racing lark Heggie you'll need to get yourself a 'near-miss' story where you can regale how close you were to nearly winning a fortune! I couldn't go to Cheltenham the year after as I was at a conference in Brighton but planned to do a Yankee.'

'Ah yes – you mentioned a Yankee bet the other day, a combination bet of four horses starting with doubles and then trebles and an accumulator,' Heggie said proudly, beaming that he was using the correct terminology.

'For me it's more fun to pick horses with large odds which could potentially lead to a large payout for a small stake. That day I picked my four horses in the morning with great pains and I remember feeling very content and optimistic that this was going to be the lucky day. That's usually the case though most mornings of a race day! I had a new boss and the company were paying me to be on the conference viewing stand rather than seeking my fortune at Ladbrokes, so I had to wait until the last moment before dashing out of the conference hall and up the main drag in Brighton to the only bookies I knew. I only visited Brighton once a year for this conference and imagine my dismay when I found that that particular Ladbrokes had closed since my last visit. I pegged it back down the hill to find another one but by the time I

125

located a William Hill's, I had missed the first two races and my first two selections had already won at 12/1 and 20/1! I was left only with the last two - which I did a small double on and they both won; Hardy Eustace at 33/1 and Maximise at 40/1. I would have won a quarter of a million quid if I had got there on time for my 50 pence each-way Yankee!'

'Ooh, I should get one of those stories for sure!' Heggie marvelled. Keith was pleased that someone for once was interested in his near-miss story.

'I now go to the races for fun, with the family now and again and with my old mates John Gronow and Frosty to Cheltenham once a year for the first day of the Festival. John's favourite expression is 'don't give it all back' if you've had had a winner. Now knowing what I do know, and having no access to any real information, I just do 10p each way Yankees. One day Heggie, one day, for my £2.20, they will all come in and I'll buy that horse and open up a sandwich bar and call it 'The Fat King sandwich bar'.'

'Why Fat King?'

'It's silly really, used to draw a picture of a Fat King on my enveloped when I wrote home to my dear old Gramps from Uni so he could see instantly that it was from me.'

'Wonderful stuff, all of it,' chuckled Heggie, 'I'll start tomorrow.'

.o0o.

I'm just connecting Heggie to Keith's fluffy, puffy, pink world. We are in a better place today. Heggie has just told Keith that he has bought him a multipack of iced gems for when he wakes up - so that is code for a long story while he munches through the six ruddy bags and only picking off the iced bits from the last two bags. When we get out of here we're heading straight for the shop to get our own pack.

.o0o.

'You asked me about marriage Keith so I thought today would be a good day to tell you, while we have some time. It's going to help me think through with something as well. No, no need to answer or get up Keith – just lay there and listen.

'I mentioned Monica and Nophelia to you before, but never got to tell you the story. I met Monica when I was staying at 'Le Suffren' hotel, Mauritius. You may have been there yourself, it's now a five star joint with 100 wonderful rooms overlooking the waterfront - but back then it was just a rundown, bohemian kinda place with 100 rooms overlooking the waterfront. I was relaxing on a stop off between Asia and Africa – I can't remember now if I was going to Africa or Asia or which one I was coming from – the old memory doesn't seem to be able to recall, must have been a traumatic event or too much booze, well there we go. Anyway, the guide book I was reading as I was sat in reception said that that hotel was an ideal stop over between the two. So, I was in the right place. Fascinating things guide books don't you think Keith?

'That is when I saw her, the most beautiful girl I had ever seen. She walked into the reception area and the sun shone through her hair, illuminating the blondeness. It was like she was moving in slow motion and the moment seemed to last at least half an hour – the whole world slowed around me. That's the only time that

127

has ever happened. Somewhere in the background, probably in my head, a tune played "I belong with you, you belong with me, my sweetheart". She came in through the large wooden, sand blasted doors and swept between the large terracotta coloured pillars. She was carrying only a small holdall and looked magnificently natural with her long flowing flouncy dress, understated brown leather sandals and with the front of her hair kept up off her face by her sunglasses. Just like the sun shone through her blonde hair, it also shone through that dress – tastefully like, but magnificent all the same. She checked in and disappeared up the staircase to her room.

'I waited in reception until she returned. She spoke in Spanish to the receptionist and the only phrase I understood was 'Raphus cucullatus', that's Latin for dodo to you Keith. Mauritius was the only known habitat of the dodo and they have a particularly fine stuffed specimen at the local museum, so the guide book I had just been reading had explained. Fantastically practical things these guide books don't you think Keith. So that was where I shot off to. I was admiring said stuffed bird when in she walked, still a picture of radiance. I wooed and wowed her with by botanical knowledge and convinced her to accompany me on the all-you-can-eat-and-drink island disco cruise from Port Louis later that evening.

'My usual demons got me and I had too much of the local vino. I ended up being left on the one of the islands the disco cruise boat stopped off at. Lucky for me, Monica also enjoyed the very same vino in about the same quantities and was marooned as well. We tried a couple of times to get off that island the next day by making rafts and the like but it was only as it approached evening the second night that we heard the music of a restaurant only about 500 meters from our little makeshift love nest under the palm trees.

'We dined on exquisite Creole dishes in the restaurant and drank a particularly potent blend of the local cocktails from the novelty bottles behind the bar before heading back to our private beach and love nest. Mauritius is only 61km long and 41km wide but it seemed like we were on our own world. We travelled together extensively over the next two years, getting lost in places you wouldn't know existed before coming back here to my country pile.

'And what about Nophelia? I hear you ask. Ah, my raven headed Nophelia. I wasn't much involved in bands at the time and I was mooching around here with Monica. We were just hanging out. I was tending the borders and the flowers and having a few drinkypoos in the garden of an afternoon. I woke up one afternoon to see these two feral looking boys disappearing behind my shed with my ham baguette I'd gotten myself for lunch, made with a little too much butter. Their skin was bronzed from the sun and their hair was dyed. It looked like they'd enjoyed every minute the summer had had to offer them and had been outside the whole time. One had a thick blonde streak down the middle of his head like a Mohican and the other had two streaks, a bit like a skunk. They both had blue jeans and Fred Perry shirts on – right little bovver boys they looked. I went to investigate but they had disappeared.

'Monica didn't believe me though, 'too much of de boozee-boozee,' she said in her pigeon English, grinning from ear to ear 'now you are imagining people in your garden'. It went on for a while, this stealing my food whilst I was asleep, but I didn't mind. If these kids needed food then I was happy to oblige. I saw them again a few times over the next few weeks, same bronzed faces, same clothes, same disappearing trick. They were sleeping rough in my sheds. I could see the cardboard they brought with them and hid behind the bushes to use later. I could see the nest areas in the sheds. I put out some blankets for them and started leaving hampers in the sheds.'

'You're going crazeee,' Monica would say, 'zeeeing these people in your garden. You need a holiday. I arrange!'

'I came face to face with them one day. There they were, standing on my path. My ham baguette in hand along with a sherbet dib-dab from the hamper.

'Gentlemen,' I said, 'are you lads okay?'

'We're fine mister,' they replied, quite sternly.

'Are you just playing or living in my garden?'

No answer.

'There's people that can help, I can call the police if you like?'

'No, just leave us alone mister, we don't want to go back there.'

'Where?'

'Brooklands.'

'That's the kiddies' home along the road there, right?'

'Yeah, we'll be gone in a week, when our Mam comes back to get us. We're okay here mister – we're not causing you any trouble.'

'I knew it Keith, I hadn't been imagining it. These kids were real. Then, from behind me, I could hear the crunching of people coming down the pebble path. The kids scarpered into the shed. So scared they were that one bumped and span me round a little in their effort to get out of

130

sight, enough that I was unbalanced and I fell hitting my head on a flowerpot. A couple of uniformed coppers came round the corner with Monica.'

'Theeze nice men are looking for some boys who ran away from zee care home down the street last week. They are door to dooring to see if anyone has seen them. I told them you big boozer. I told them you have been seeing people in your garden.'

'Now Keith, I had a pretty big decision to make. Dob these kids in who were cowering in the shed all but a couple of feet behind me so they could be returned and looked after in the system – not what they wanted for certain, but possibly the best for them, or say nothing and in doing so, breaking the law.'

'I took a deep breath. 'I feel like Eric Clapton,' I announced. He knew he had hit rock bottom when he couldn't fish one day. Stood there on the bank he was, so pie-eyed that he couldn't tie his hook or cast out, let alone get his luncheon meat and maggot combination presented appropriately.'

'The Policemen looked at me very strangely, spread-eagled on the floor and wedged between some flowerpots. I had to translate. 'I'm just a drunk,' I said. 'Just a drunk who can't even stand up, who can't even do his gardening no more. I could see one of the boys had dropped his dib-dab and the police saw it too. 'I'm just a drunk who likes dib-dabs and needs a holiday. I'll show you around the garden and the sheds if you want to have a look for these kids – the sheds up at the back away from the house are your best bets. Help me up would you?

'I led the Police up and around the garden. The kids hid somewhere else and didn't get caught. I packed up three big hampers for them, enough to last them the week they thought they would be around for – and some, and went on holiday.

'I had always wanted to travel to Egypt and see the pyramids and the Sphinx and this was the destination of the holiday on which Monica had booked me. Monica didn't want to go as there was some sort of problem when she was last there. She said she had met a 'horrible geezer'. I don't know sometimes when she is punning or not. Monica's college friend, Nophelia, lived out there and had married a Scandinavian business man. Monica told me that they had been extremely close until she met this man and, although I would receive a warm welcome from Nophelia, the man was sure to be grumpy - but I wasn't to mind him too much. Monica sent me off with an address scribbled on a bit of paper, a letter she told me was written in ancient Arabic and would see me through any tight spots and a wedge of Egyptian currency. I told her I was rather going to use my credit card but she told me this was unlikely to be of any use in the places where Nophelia was going to take me and I was likely to be travelling a fair old way. She emphasised the words 'a fair old way' and laughed - it sounded like 'a pharaoh way', but again, I wasn't sure if she was punning.

'I took a cruise down the Nile having arrived on a very nice flight from Heathrow. The heat was something I hadn't experienced before, a particularly dry heat. I was out on deck having a cigarette in the sun when the ship's doctor advised me that I should be careful smoking in such a dry heat. 'It will set the tar in your chest solid you know,' he told me. He explained that the locals always smoked in the shade and gave it a little time before going back out in the sun and they mixed 'camsphill', that's camel spit Keith don't you know, with their tobacco to provide some lasting moisture. 'The biggest cause of death for outside workers in Egypt,' the doctor went on, 'is the tar setting like tarmac in the lungs. Particularly harmful for westerners like yourself, not acclimatised to the dryness and heat of the climate. I suggest you use the climate controlled smoking room on the first deck, if you have to smoke at all that is – very bad for one's health,' and with that, he lit his pipe, billowed a large plume of smoke from his lungs and wandered off.

'I met up with Nophelia and her grumpy husband, Sven. Her existence was miserable. Sven was a bore and a pig. I expect Monica knew this and had sent me on some sort of mercy mission. Sven had taken a job in Egypt many years ago, knowing he was terminally ill. He had snared Nophelia quickly with a charm he had since managed to dispose of and he had vented his ailment related frustrations on her ever since. I don't know why she stayed with him as she was a stunner, very alluring, and in fact, I'm convinced that she could have had any man that she would have wanted.

'Sven chain smoked and the house reeked of tobacco. He never told Nophelia that he smoked before they married; in fact he went beyond to keep it hidden from her. Nophelia's father had died a very painful death from lung cancer and it would have been a deal breaker in the marriage stakes. He smoked crafty ciggies all the time and, at first, he would give it a few hours of abstinence before he saw her so she couldn't smell it on him. Once they were married, he smoked more - but around the outside of the house, always making an excuse like putting the rubbish out or closing the shed door. He was a

133

crafty one. He brushed his teeth afterwards and rinsed with mouthwash. Actually, his oral hygiene was something that Nophelia thought was pretty nice about him. The piles of butts that built up in little hidden pockets around the house required some serious cleansing from time to time, plus efficient disposal - not in the normal rubbish as they smelt too much, but double wrapped in bags and taken to nearby bins. Then he seemed to care less about hiding it and purposely let the sordid habit be discovered. He didn't care; he had no respect and brought the smoking into the house, into the bedroom. She begged him to give up, but when he wouldn't, she begged him just to take it outside, but he wouldn't – the rotter and absolute cad.

'Sven's cough had gotten worse and he was now unable to go out much. When he did, he seemed to delight in embarrassing Nophelia in front of everyone he possibly could - he had such a lack of respect for her. Now, I'm no husband of the year, but the golden rule as far as I'm concerned is never to embarrass your wife in public

'I suggested to Nophelia that we went to the pyramids together one day and take a trip down into one of the inner chambers where the Pharaoh's were buried with their possessions, slaves and crocodile parts. You didn't know that Keith, did you, that they buried parts of crocodiles that would come alive when the tomb was sealed to protect the Pharaoh. I invited the crocodile, even thought this ridiculously grumpy man was a menace and I had taken an instant dislike to his rudeness. Not wishing to miss an opportunity to be cruel to the lovely Nophelia, he agreed that he would attend.

'Funnily enough, even though he had lived in the country for a good many years, he had never been to the pyramids before. He said he viewed this as a tawdry, tourist and dusty affair, whatever that meant. He showed a lack of respect even to the country, the people and their heritage.

'The air was dampish down in the pyramid and Sven commented that it eased his breathing. No sooner had we cramped our way down the long flight of steps with bent backs and doubled-up knees to the first chamber that Sven lit one of his awful cigarettes. The guide asked him to extinguish the cigarette but he flatly refused. He smoked it down to the butt, blowing out great clouds of the stinky smoke, alternately back up the stairway and in the general direction of Nophelia. How could any sane and mildly nice person think it was okay to smoke in the middle of a pyramid – I ask you! I asked him if his bad chest had anything to do with the fags and he assured me, brusquely, that it was certainly not. I have to admit Keith, from what the doctor had told me on the cruise ship, I knew he would be in trouble once he went back out into the dryness and heat of the desert – no camel spit in sight you see. I sort of encouraged him, in a reverse psychological way, to have another cigarette before we climbed back up the stairs, by asking him not to smoke again and ruin it for everyone else on the tour. He did just what I thought he would do and lit up instantly.

'When poor old Sven stepped out from the pyramid through his cloud of smoke, it seemed like someone was laying a layer of bitumen on the inside of his lungs, right down to the very last ventricle. You may not be aware of this Keith, but if you were to fold out all the surface area of the insides of the lungs, the bits that take the oxygen in, it would spread out to at least two football

135

fields. He kinda seized up, gasping for air, as if he was solidifying and turning to stone. He became more rigid. He kinda went into slow motion and keeled over. I had no idea that his lungs were so full of tar and that they would set so quickly. I thought it would be amusing to see him struggle a bit, but I wasn't expecting that. You should never attack anyone, however justified you feel, unless you have calculated the cost of winning.

'His nearest, and possibly the one who loved him most, Nophelia had little remorse for his death - so I shouldn't really feel that guilty. Sad state of affairs when your closest beloved doesn't feel the pain.   But there you have it Keith, I suppose I'm responsible for someone's actual demise, even though I don't think he had long to go anyway.

'Nophelia came with me back to England. We got back through the borders quickly with the cash and the letter written in Arabic, which I later found out translated as 'the bearer of this letter is an English Doctor seeking herbal remedies to an unknown and rather contagiously rampant form of bright purple rash which appeared on his bottom one day whilst Morris Dancing in Stow under the Wold'.'

Part 2

The Journey to the Fat King Music Listening Studios

Chapter 20

In Pursuit of the Ultimate 400 Meters Freestyle, Part 5 (The Reckoning)

The programme for the club champs was out. Twelve weeks to go but there would be no Dad's race.

Keith watched the masters train that Saturday morning. It was decision time. Up the ante or stop thinking he was good. Keith joined the masters and booked his first training session.

It was another come-uppance. Keith couldn't keep pace with anyone really. They didn't have the rest intervals that he and Ben had when they did their sessions. He couldn't get his breath, got cramp and struggled at the back of the lane.

The coach offered some helpful cramp related advice. 'Vitamin C and lots of fluids.'

Keith thought the prospect of taking vitamins was a bit old age related but was happy to give it a go.

The sage of the masters' lane, even older than Keith, suggested tonic water for the quinine.

'I could do gin and tonics,' said Keith.

'Only the tonic though,' the sage clarified.

Keith persevered. He focussed on the reason he was doing this - for the adrenaline rush Heggie had spoken about, for the fitness Katy said would be good, because he should have a target as per Alan, and he wanted to keep the dream alive before it was too late like Steve.

Keith completed his entry form, much to the delight of his children, filled out a cheque to cover the cost of his races, after calculating the penny per metre ratio, and returned it to a somewhat surprised coach who looked after the masters swimmers.

The deed was done. He would compete first in the 200 individual medley and then in the 400m front crawl.

Keith trained two sessions each week with the masters and another session, if time allowed, on his own.

He used his resistance cords appropriately.

Keith thought about a taper in his training schedule so he was ready to compete well on the day but then remembered that he hadn't actually done enough training to warrant tapering. He decided the only taper he could effect, was to reduce the amount of red wine consumed in the run up to event day.

In the pool, Keith concentrated on building up enough strength to make a 50 meters fly, which was the first part of the individual medley. Fly comes with its own complications for swimmers of a certain age. The tremendous effort required to pull the body forward with both arms going at the same time is demanding enough for most people; but to race it could cause serious and lasting damage for the more mature swimmer.

Race day, and with excitement and trepidation, Keith packed his children's competition bags – goggles, swim hats, trunks and costumes, snacks, drinks, club t-shirts, shorts, spare goggles, spare swim hats, spare costumes and extra towels. Keith put his competition bag together – goggles, trunks and a towel. He tightened his goggles to race tightness, picked out his best pair of trunks, checking for holes or see-through bits and popped a towel in his bag.

The pool looked magnificent. As it was race day it was laid out in the full 50 meters, anti-wave lane ropes, starting blocks, electronic finishing pads, the electronic score board, the 5 meter flags for the backstroke and the 10 meter false start rope. Not a ripple was on the water as the boys were invited to do their warm up. Six beautiful lanes.

Keith took it easy during the warm up; no point overdoing things this close to the race. The usual aches in the shoulders were there; but no other new complications thank goodness.

The swimmers were given 10 minutes use of the full pool before a couple of lanes were dedicated to the swimmers who wanted to practice their starts and sprints. Keith lined up ready to go off the blocks with the other swimmers. It was reassuring that there were a number of other masters competing and they were all trying out their dives.

The boys cleared the pool and the girls took their turn to warm up. The boys warmed up first as it was a boy's event first, the 200 Individual Medley.

Keith was in heat three, lane one. The entry time Keith made up was 2 minutes 50 seconds and some 6 seconds off the club record for the 40 – 44 year olds. Keith felt he had a chance of getting the club record - but hadn't told anyone apart from his family through fear of sensational failure.

He was mindful that anything could happen during his first swim in so long. Keith had set himself a number of benchmarks:

firstly, it would be good if he finished without having to be hauled out by the lifeguard after a heart attack;

secondly, it would be great if his trunks and goggles stayed on during the dive;

thirdly, it would be excellent if he kept a good, fast pace and maintained his stroke technique and didn't turn into a jellyfish looking geriatric; and

finally, and the one he hoped for most after not having a heart attack; it would be brilliant if he managed to break the club record for his age group.

Surely he could? He had timed himself in training and he was near. He had swum a 2 minutes 11 seconds in this pool when he was a young man, so a 2 minutes 44 surely was possible...... What Keith naturally assumed, wasn't in fact, fact. There is no real correlation between what you used to do and what you can do now, given the passing of time, with no real training and hammering your body, hard, for the last 20 or so years.

Keith went down to the oddly called 'whipping area' where the swimmers assemble and are put into heat and lane order. No actual whipping takes place however some shouting is required by the 'whips' to get 40 or so excited swimmers into their correct positions. Keith's heat was assembled.

The whip reminded Keith he was in lane one and helpfully told him they put the old boys next to the wall as it was easier to get them out during the race if anything went wrong. Keith's competitors were at least half Keith's age, some were more than half.

Heat one, consisting of the more junior swimmers, went through the passageway from the changing rooms onto poolside. The announcer introduced the event and the heat and handed over to the referee. Keith's tummy turned. The referee called them to their marks, the beep of the gun sounded and there was a splash as they dived into the pool. Keith's tummy turned again.

The next heat went though, including Ford. Keith's tummy turned for Ford and turned for himself.

Keith's heat filed up to the exit of the whipping area. From the whipping area corridor, Keith could now see the pool. The referee called Ford's heat to their marks and off they went on the sound of the beep. It helped Keith to watch Ford. It took his mind off his race. Keith was shaking though with nerves.

Keith's heat filed onto poolside and the balcony of spectators came into view. It was a mildly amusing sideshow for the spectators to see masters swimmers competing amongst the normal competition. It was a mildly amusing sideshow for the officials to see the masters swimmers competing. As fellow parents, I'm sure they all wanted Keith to swim well. A number of the officials commented to Keith how brave they thought he was. This did nothing to help Keith.

Keith watched Ford finish his race. Keith's mind was now white with competition; part fear, part nerves, part adrenalin. The largest part was fear.

Silence fell across the pool.

'Just keep it together, relax,' Keith thought to himself.

The referee blew three short blasts on his whistle to mark the start of the next heat preparations. Keith's stomach turned a further three times and his body released a massive wave of adrenaline which made his head go hot and nearly lose control of his bowels.

The announcer hailed, 'heat three of the men's 200 Individual Medley, over to you Mr Referee'.

The referee completed his long, final whistle and raised his arm offering the swimmers to climb up onto their blocks. Keith climbed up, a little wobbly as his legs were very jelly. Keith settled into his start position.

'Relax, don't go early and remember to do butterfly first,' Keith said to himself.

Mr Referee offered the start to the starter.

'Take your marks.'

'Wait, don't move, wait for the beep.'

BEEP!

Keith pulled down on the blocks slightly and threw his arms out in front of himself, pushing with his legs. Stuck in the 1980's, Keith had elected to start with both feet on the front of the blocks whereas all the other swimmers used a track start with their feet staggered. This, coupled with the slow reaction time and the height needed to effect an old boy hitch-kick in mid air, meant that Keith was into the water last. His body mass however and the angle of entry allowed Keith to catch up.

'Good, goggles and trunks stayed on. Kick, kick, kick, arm pull and first stroke. Don't look over, do your own thing.'

The race had started well and Keith settled into his butterfly stroke. Two pulls and one breath.

At 25 meters Keith's stroke was fluid and the shoulders felt fine.

'This is feeling better than I thought, keep it going Keith.'

Into the second 25 meters of the race. Keith had planned to keep it steady for the 50 meters butterfly.

'This isn't hurting as much as expected; I think I could increase the pace a little. This could be better than I thought.'

Keith turned in a relatively fast time of 33 seconds and, not that it mattered particularly as the other people in Keith's heat were teenagers and not in his age group, he was in first place.

'That's going to hurt,' one of the coaches on poolside said.

Keith turned onto the backstroke leg of the medley.

'Ow, that's starting to hurt, I've gone out too fast. Fool. Breathe deeply, get some oxygen in.'

Keith started to struggle on the second half of the backstroke leg.

'Keep it together, hold the stroke, get ready for the breaststroke.'

Keith changed his backstroke stroke rate so that he could turn on his best arm, well the only arm we was any good at turning on. Swimmers have to remain on their back in the backstroke leg of the Individual Medley at all times until they touch the wall. In pure backstroke events, you are able to roll onto your front and turn – much easier.

'Keep the technique Keith.'

For the breaststroke transition, swimmers are allowed to take one full arm pull down to the side of their body and one full leg kick before the head needs to break the surface of the water. Swimming underwater breaststroke can be faster; especially when coupled with a good push off the wall. It's a big ask though, particularly half way through the medley as the swimmer spends quite a time underwater, especially when they've already built up an oxygen debt and a large quantity of lactic acid in the muscles. Keith planned to take advantage of the underwater pull but would keep it short.

Keith pushed off the wall.

'Forget the pull – you won't make it. No don't forget the pull – it will be faster.'

Keith's lungs were burning half way through the underwater arm pull.

'You're not going to make it to the surface you fool.'

Keith bobbed up and tried to get into his stroke.

'Use your legs, kick, kick.'

The pain was intense. He hadn't the lung capacity to get the oxygen into his lungs which his muscles needed. The muscles were burning and crying out for oxygen. The oxygen was impeded by the lung damage and the tar. The lactic acid was building up and his arms were as sore as the day after he had done the first stretch cord session. The other swimmers were gaining on him and would be level in a few meters.

'It will be okay, onto the front crawl next and your best stroke.'

Keith could see his children at the end of the lane cheering him on. He hoped he didn't look too much of a mess.

'Hit the turn hard, two hand touch, shoulders level, drop the elbow, knees up, other arm over, push, kick, streamline.'

This sequence happened in exactly the way Keith called it, but to anyone who was watching it seemed to happen in slow motion.

'Pull, stretch out the stroke, catch and build into it.'

The transition into the front crawl was textbook. It just took a long time. The other swimmers powered away on the front crawl and Keith managed the return leg front crawl in 40 seconds. He thought the front crawl was his forte, but it was poor.

It was shock, a shock to Keith and a shock to his body. He missed the club record and he was soundly beaten by a number of younger swimmers. He had also debilitated himself somewhat. He sure had felt an adrenaline rush like he hadn't felt for 20 years. He sure felt pain in his arms and shoulders like he hadn't felt for 20 years.

The 400 meters front crawl followed a similar pattern. Keith went out at a reasonable pace, great stroke count, but had nothing left in the tank. He was sensationally overtaken by a 13 year old on the last length. With nothing else to give, he tried to keep his stroke and finish as solidly as he could. Panting at the end was an understatement.

Keith had been taught a lesson. It was evident. He hadn't come up to his own expectations. He wasn't upset though with the good performance he hadn't achieved after not putting the work in. He resolved that he would train harder and things would be different the next swimming competition he entered.

Chapter 21

Cracked it!

It had taken a good number of years trying to actually happen. For Keith, it was fortunate. Many punters would never experience a large win on the horses; but Keith did, not long after telling Heggie all about the races.

'Cracked it! I've cracked it this time! I'm in! Four winners darling wife, love of my life!' Keith cried, hugging and dancing his wife around the kitchen. 'My tidily Yankee on this damp afternoon has paid us big dividends.'

'Well done darling, how much have we won!' Katy said, rubbing her hands together in delight and thinking it might be enough to cover a really nice meal out or even a weekend away. Keith had been betting these bets for so long now with so many near misses that she wasn't holding her breath.

'I've tried to work it out and I think it will be over a hundred grand! I won't know until I've picked it up. I can take a year off contracting! Yahoo! No more trains. I might even open up my sandwich bar! I'll be home before 4 o'clock every day! More time to spend with you and the kids darling, you lucky old thing. Look, look at the results,' said Keith pointing at the text on the TV screen.

'I'm very excited for you. Well done. They won't pay you in cash will they? I don't want you walking around with that kind of money!' his concerned wife said.

'They'll pay me by cheque I would imagine, unless I insist on cash, but I'll ask Heggie to come with me to make sure I'm safe and I'll go straight to the bank to make the deposit.'

'You better go and find him pretty quick then, I imagine the bookmakers will be closing at six.'

Keith strode down the garden, at least 10 feet tall. There was something new and exciting outside the shed. It had a note attached:

The sun-ergiser! An invention by Hector Pump. Dear Keith, please find attached to this note the prototype of the sun-ergiser. Designed to allow you to sit in the sun without the wind! Go on, take a seat and enjoy!

Keith was amused by the 'please find attached to this note...' part. Usually the expression was reserved for items of a relatively equal size. The 'sun-ergiser' stood over six feet tall and six feet long. It consisted of two fence panels set the width of a chair apart with a wooden back so the three sides enclosed the recliner placed within. It looked like a gigantic filled waffle. The whole construction was set upon two disks, one on the ground and one on the base of the parts, so the whole unit could be rotated – presumably in the direction of the sun and away from the wind. Keith rotated the contraption in line with the sun and settled into the recliner, noticing that it had been branded in marker pen ©HectorPump on the inside.

It worked. The sun threw down the rays which were received strongly and without wind. Keith nodded off in the cocoon like space and was asleep in under 2 minutes. His brain kicked in as it didn't like to hang around and he was awake and up three minutes later.

Keith pushed his way through the hedge. Heggie was thrilled at the news and congratulated Keith heartily.

'You certainly have cracked it!

'Look at this Heggie. Bahati at 20/1, Boo at 40/1, Ford Pollard at 33/1 and to top it all, Lady Bahai, the rank outsider in the race romped home by a short head at 25/1. Keith 1, Bookies 0.'

'Poor old bookmaker,' said Heggie as they danced around the shed together, 'I hope he laid some of it off to cover his losses. I would be delighted to be your bodyguard and accompany you to the bookmakers.'

'I'll get the loose change in cash and I'll buy you a beer Heggie at the Chequers for your fine help and by way of a celebration, why damn it, I'll buy you a snack as well!'

'He's lying down in the back room,' said the young girl in the bookmakers through her bubble gum. 'He told me to tell you to go straight through,' she added without looking up from her mobile phone and scratching off lunch from her black leggings.

'Classy chick,' whispered Heggie.

'She's a wrong 'un that one,' whispered Keith back.

The security door was clicked open by the girl and they went through the small, brown formica lined hallway to the back office to see the man who was laid down. The walls were stained with tobacco and the air stank of stale cigarettes.

'The smoking ban in the workplace hasn't reached these parts yet then,' whispered Keith.

'I'm ruined,' came the sorry voice from the manager's office. It was Eddie Brazil, the owner. 'I'll come straight out with it. Your bet has ruined me. Can I pay you in instalments? I can give you

149

£8,583.50 now and can we agree £10,000 per month for the next ten months?'

'Now just a minute,' started Heggie, 'a bet is a bet!'

'Please, I just need time to get back on my feet!' pleaded Eddie. 'I'm good for it – it's just a cash flow situation, that's all.'

'Okay,' said Keith, 'it's a deal. I'll have the £83.50 in cash please as I wish to by my friend here a pint and a pie and I'll have the £8,500 in a cheque.'

'You must be mad,' said Heggie as Eddie turned his back and fumbled through the draws of his decrepit desk for his chequebook. He yanked hard at the stuck drawer until it opened. He wrote out the cheque shaking his head and handed it over with a shaky hand.

Eddie Brazil didn't look much like a successful bookmaker, or a successful anything really. He was thin and timid and his scrawny back was still hunched as he leant to one side to take some money out of his trouser pocket. He burnt his other hand on the cigarette which he had stood up on its butt and on his desk and he yelped and knocked over the contents of the full ashtray into his lap. It looked from the state of the front of his trousers that this was not the first time he had done that that day. Brushing himself down, he unfurled four twenty pound notes from his pocket and said he was going to get the three pounds and 50p from the till.

'He only has a £50,000 guarantee,' whispered Keith as Eddie was out of the room, 'I'll take my chances on getting all of it rather than just half of it or none at all if I was to bankrupt him!'

'Here, the three pounds and fifty,' said Eddie, hunching his way back into the office. 'I'll see you anytime after the first of the month. I'm here all of the time, just see the girl on the front desk and she'll let you through. Thanks for your understanding. I'm just having a run of bad luck that's all.'

'Come on, I'll buy you that drink,' ushered Keith.

'No, I'll buy you that drink, that's a real downer for you!'

Classy chick was on her phone when they left the bookmakers, whispering in hushed tones into the handset. Keith couldn't quite hear all of what she was saying but the bits he did hear were: 'Yeah, him, the one who rides his bike......, helmet taped up with black tape.... with that weirdo.... lays in his flower beds.' She hung up without looking up at them as they left.

The Chequers was a drinking pub with a Chinese take-away included, occupying an imposing location in the village opposite the convenience store, the barbers and the fish and chip shop. The village boasted a good number of pubs within walking distance of the Chequers but it was the closest to the bookies and Keith and Heggie's houses. Keith had only been in there a few times before and it always seemed that there was an edge to the place. Once, two men had had an argument across Keith as he stood at the bar waiting to be served. A colossal man was nicely asking another smallish man to settle a debt. Keith thought it would not be appropriate to move in case he inflamed the situation, so the row went on around him for quite some time. The smallish man held his ground, only let himself down when he choked with fear a few moments later on his gin and tonic. It was common knowledge that all the previously banned people had come back to the pub when it changed hands.

Keith and Heggie settled down at the corner table and made a start into the loose change of the winnings. The furniture and the clientele were not dissimilar in their diversity. Different designs, an odd assortment of shapes and sizes clothed in an array of fabric; fleece mainly. The furniture was the same. The heavily embossed emulsion washed wallpaper sat above, but didn't interact with, the intensely varnished cheap pine lining the bottom half of the walls.

'Why the deal Keith? Why not insist on the lot or take the guaranteed £50,000?' Heggie asked.

The late evening sun was partly blocked by the horizontal tin blinds, salvaged from some 1970's municipal building. The rows of light shone onto the poorly assembled faux wooden beams and the clumsy new screw-heads proud above the planks. The light was shining into Keith's eyes, so he shifted his position closer to the pile of garden umbrellas leant between the stained big screen roller blind and the cheap radiator.

'I'm not sure that gambling debts are even enforceable in English law, guarantees or no guarantees. I know that's certainly the case on at a racecourse. There are numerous failed bookmakers who haven't settled their debt and no-one likes a stinker do they. I wouldn't want to particularly do that to the poor old chap that is Eddie Brazil. I think it's my best chance to get the money. Eddie Brazil stays afloat so he's happy. My Gramps and I have been going to that bookies for years now and I'm not sure I want him going to the one in Great Missenden anyway should this one close down. Let's think of it as my commitment to community work as I can't see another bookies opening up if that one closes. Look what happened to Threshers, it is now a charity shop. We can't have two charity shops in the village, them in Great Missenden would laugh even more at us! One sometimes has to set one's stall out and be reasonable.'

'Why did you chose 'Bahati',' asked Heggie.

'I thought it would be fun shouting it over the finishing line. Go on Bahati.'

'Why Boo?'

'My father-in-law calls Carina 'Boo'. I've been following it for a while.'

'I can see why you chose Ford Pollard.'

'Yes, I saw it run last time out at Windsor. It lost 15 lengths at the start, ran wide and only finished last by one length. This time it ran on a right handed track so had the rails to guide it rather than the figure of 8 track at Windsor. And as for Lady Bahai, our hotel in Tenerife was called the Bahai Princess, such lovely imagery don't you think. It was listed to run yesterday and didn't so I thought the owners and trainers really wanted to run it soon as they entered it for two races. It costs money to enter races so I thought it was a bit lavish entering two so closely together.'

'Nice reasoning on all points,' said Heggie.

Dark forces were at play in the usually sleepy village of Prestwood. The local Robinson brothers were also in the Chequers that afternoon. The only other punter was a heavily tattooed man occupying the stool at the far end of the bar, keeping himself to himself. The area's hoodlum count had risen to 3.

The Robinson brothers sat in silence drinking their lager tops. An electronic dog barked to signify a mobile phone was ringing and one of the Robinson brothers hit the answer button and they both listened through the speaker.

'Hi sis, how's it going?' Robinson brother number one said loudly and the brothers both chuckled at their own ringtone joke.

The ostentation at having a mobile phone conversation broadcast riled the barman and he flounced out. The tattooed man listened with interest but showed no response to their antics.

'That's interesting,' Robinson brother number one said quietly, now picking up the phone and turning it off speaker. He turned slightly towards Keith and Heggie as he took the information in his sister was relaying. 'That much? First of each month, understood. Thanks for the update.'

It wasn't difficult to identify the man who laid in his flower beds she had described in her call earlier, he was fairly well known in the village. The news of a big win was interesting to them; especially in a rival bookmakers. The target would have been weakened from a large payout. On receipt of the new news, the target had changed.

Robinson brother number one whispered for a few moments to his brother and then they both slid from their seats and approached Heggie and Keith.

'Congratulations,' said Robinson brother number one as both of them sat down at Heggie and Keith's table.

Keith coughed into his beer through a mix of surprise and fright. He didn't want anything to do with the Robinson Brothers.

'Good news travels fast; let me get you another round to celebrate,' the Robinson brother continued.

'No thanks,' said Heggie rather bravely, 'private drink,' he went on, rather courageously.

Keith's heart leapt up into his throat and then back down into his stomach. He didn't want to be centre of attention - conflict with people in the village was not the sort of thing he wished for.

'You've got yourself a bad deal,' Robinson brother number two said firmly.

Keith clenched his buttocks firmly so he didn't follow through.

'You should know a bad deal,' said Heggie, suicidally, 'you've been giving bad deals out for a while.'

'Okay, I'll cut to the chase. We'll give you all the money owed to you right now if you give us that betting slip,' the first Robinson brother went on, 'everyone's a winner.'

Keith prepared to speak. The lump in his throat made it difficult.

'Except the bookie,' Heggie said helpfully, now seemingly intent on a kamikaze mission, 'what's in it for him?'

'Crikey Heggie,' thought Keith, *'don't make it any worse here for us! The bookie is on his own on this one!'*

'Retirement,' sneered Robinson brother two, 'we'll take on his bet and honour your winnings. We'll offer him a good rate of interest or, he can sell up to us.'

'Sometimes, in life,' Heggie went on, much to Keith's dismay, 'you have to set your stall out. My friend here was just telling me about his integrity – he's made the deal and he won't go back on it.'

'I don't want to know about all this,' thought Keith to himself, wishing to avoid any conflict in his life, and in particular with anyone from the village. Keith's simple 'beat the bookies' game was about to cause misery to one hunchy bookmaker and would condone the act of nasty business dealings.

Seeing Keith was reasoning on the softer side of the deal they had proposed, Robinson brother number one provided some comforting reason.

'It's only business, pure and simple.'

Keith hadn't managed to get a word out yet.

'No,' Keith said firmly. 'The deal is done. I'm a man of honour,' which in hindsight, Keith thought, wasn't the best thing to have said as it implied the Robinson's weren't. He surprised himself with his response.

'The offer is still there if you want to reconsider – you have until the first of the month to decide I understand,' was Robinson brother number one's reasonable response and he rose and left Heggie and Keith to their drinks, pulling his brother up with him.

'I expected them to say something like 'it's your funeral,' as a parting shot or something equally sinister,' said Keith 'I think we got off lightly!'

'Come on,' said Heggie, 'it's time to go, my pants are a bit damp.'

The Robinson Brothers returned to the bar.

'What the hell was all that about?'

'What do you mean?'

'Have you gone soft or something?'

'Soft, me?'

'A bit of Robinson persuasion would have gotten us that betting slip.'

'Do you know who he is?'

'I'm not into hero worship. That could have been our second bookies dear brother, if you would have applied even the minutest of pressure, couldn't you see that he was bricking it?'

'Have you any recollection?' Robinson brother number one paused for his sibling's answer.

'Told you, no. Why would I know the bloke with the winnings. Hardly likely to move in my circles is he?'

'Not him, the other one – the Jim Morrison lookalike.'

'Him neither. What is this? Who's your friend game show?'

'No, didn't think you did. We are nothing but common criminals if we have no honour, now drink your drink and leave the thinking to me, bozo.'

The heavily tattooed man stood outside the Chequers pub and watched two men, a normal looking fellow and a hippy in a leather jacket, bolt through the doors, across the car park and down the road.

He took two phones from his pocket and made a call on one. The phone beeped as it engaged, there was a click and he said 'hi cellmate.'

'Don't call me that dickhead,' came the reply, in broad American. 'England's such a small place they record all of the phone calls. What news?'

'I've got the name of the place you require. It's taken me a while as the target has been low profile for such a long time.'

'Don't give me that shit. You're a thug, not a detective. I should have paid more and hired someone who knew what they were doing. You've had a good holiday on my expenses. Anyway, you've done it and that pleases me.'

'Talking of money, you can transfer the rest of the fee into my account now and I'll text you the name of the location.'

The tattooed man listened to the click of the keyboard at the other end of the line. He watched the screen of the other phone. It beeped and he read the display, 'New deposit received'.

'Thank you,' the tattooed man said and tapped in the location and sent the text.

'Okay, good work, when are you heading back?'

'Soon, I've spotted a bonus business opportunity with an acquaintance of the target.'

'Don't go messing up my plan now you clumsy fool, d'ya hear? It's too important – I don't want you drawing any attention.'

'Now you're just hurting my feelings calling me a fool. The deal was for me to find the target – what I do now is my business. You've had enough from me – even part of my ear; we're done,' he said as he rubbed the rough edges of the top of his ear. The tattooed man clicked the button on his phone to end the call, held the car key he had taken off the bar whilst the brothers were playing the big hoods, and pressed the remote button. A car clicked open.

'It had to be the stupid looking one, didn't it?'

He opened the door and slid into the driver's seat of the Robinson's car.

Chapter 22

It cracked

After another day in the big smoke, Keith was on the train home. He had caught the 6.03pm from London Marylebone, his preferred train, and had spent a very comfortable 46 minutes with a double seat to himself and a couple of cold cans of Carlsberg. Cold beer was just the thing for a sunny day and after a long day 'polishing the poo' in the office - the business technical term applied to the act of making the workings of an organisation appear a bit better than they actually were, especially when that organisation was facing an inspection or an audit.

As the train pulled out of Amersham station, one stop before Great Missenden, Keith started his packing up routine. He drained the last segment of his beer from the can and placed it in the empty plastic bag from the Off Licence. As the bag was branded with 'Amjad's wine and beer Emporium, London', he pulled out a spare from his rucksack which would hide the contents and the plastic based advertisement when he forced it into the bin next to the train doors. To stop the cans from sounding like they were empty beer cans, he folded his now read Evening Standard between them.

Keith applied some Lipsyl to his dehydrated lips, popped in a headache and a decongestant tablet and washed this down with some water before taking a milk thistle capsule to be kind to his liver. He rubbed on some antibacterial hand gel to mask the tobacco smell and combined a full strength menthol gum with a decongestant lozenge – the winning combination to make one's breath smell nice and unblock the sinuses. For good measure he took a squirt of nasal spray hoping that it would ultimately reach his blocked ears and took out a tissue in preparation for the sneeze that was sure to follow. As a precaution, he took an indigestion table as the bike ride up the hill was likely to invigorate the force fed beer in his stomach.

Keith checked his watch. *'Mmm, 6.49pm,'* he said to himself. It was the first day of the month and Keith was looking forward to collecting his first instalment.

Although the advent of evening racing usually meant that bookies stayed open later, he only had 26 minutes to get there - but he was on course. Keith was cycling up the hill. He peddled up on the footpath for the first 100 yards until the hill rose steeply at which point he had to get off the bike and walk. His brother-in-law's racer only had ten gears and Keith just didn't have the legs for it. It made him look a bit of a fool going so slowly or when he had to push the bike with his cycle gear on, but over the course of the journey, it was better than walking.

As the hill started to flatten out, he remounted and started to make up the ground he had lost on the walking commuters due to the time consuming assembly of his high-vis jacket, helmet, lights, tucking his sock into his trouser and taking the lock off the bike. As the path flattened out even more at the top of the hill, Keith had made enough speed up to change into second gear and rejoin the road at the junction opposite the Traveller's Rest. This was a tricky part of the journey as in the late summer, the sun started to set directly at the end of the road, dazzling all drivers and particularly the old ones who were too short to make use of their sun visors. This is why

160

Keith went to so much trouble on these bright summer evenings to be seen, even if those sat outside the pub thought his appearance peculiar and perhaps a little amusing.

Then an extraordinary thing happened, Keith knew it would one day. He heard a car pulling out of the Traveller's Rest car park, revving up too much and grinding the clutch. *'Know any other good tunes,'* Keith giggled to himself, *'must be an old biddy trying to find first gear!'* Keith could tell the car was going quite fast and was getting fairly close now from the roar of the engine - but he was comforted by his high visibility jacket, flashing lights and his helmet.

The car got nearer and nearer and started to unnerve Keith. He knew had a number of escape routes - onto the pavement being one of them. Keith took a backwards glance and thought that it might be safer on the pavement. Safe on the pavement, Keith slowed a little and prepared one of his best stern stares. Employing his best stern stare, Keith saw that he was not alone on the pavement; the car had followed him and was still coming.

'The driver must be having a heart attack, that's it. Pedal faster Keith', Keith said to himself. He made no distance on the car. *'Back on the road, that will be the safest place!'* Keith peddled back onto the road but the car veered onto the road again. *'I think they must have regained consciousness and straightened up, that's it, back onto the pavement!'*

There was a three-way pile up back on the pavement between the car, Keith on his bike and a little old lady who was reading the notices in the newsagent window. The car swerved back onto the road again and continued for a while before stopping.

161

Keith could feel pain in the back of his head and wished he had gone a grade higher with his crash helmet. Keith could hear loud breathing and flapping, similar to, he imagined, a large carp would make when out of water. Keith wasn't able to breathe though.

'Oh my goodness, my chest has been ripped open and I'm not getting any oxygen,' screamed Keith in his mind. He forced his eyes open, fearing that he would see his ribs and blood everywhere. It was the old lady who was doing all of the flappy breathing and she was on top of him, face to face. 'I'm okay!' he shouted with glee, 'yes, I'm okay, ha-ha!' He had a very good view of her cheeks being drawn in as if she was choking on something and spittle was being breathed out and retracted in a long dangle as she did so, right above his face. On the outward dangle, the spittle was a mere centimetre away from his nose.

'False teeth,' Keith cried, feeling embarrassed that he had shown such delight that he was in one piece and not looking to help the little old lady who was clearly in a distressed and problematic state, 'she's choking on her false teeth!'

Keith pushed her off his chest and rolled her over onto the pavement. He hesitated for a moment. *'Do I really have to put my fingers in there?'* he thought, looking at the rasping and hairy mouthpiece. The old lady cheeks were still flapping in and out. Her eyes were fixed on Keith and appeared to be screaming, *'I know it's not going to be pleasant for you - but bloody well get on with it you idiot!'*

Keith reluctantly put his fingers into her mouth. 'Eewee,' he said out loud as he did the deed. He was on top of her now to get more purchase, reaching down her throat. *'She has no teeth, I can't feel any teeth!'* he thought.

'Have you got any teeth?' he shouted.

The old lady tried to shake her head, which was quite a difficult thing to do when you have someone resting on your chest with their fingers stuck firmly down your throat.

'But there's something in here, right? I can feel something in here.'

The old girl nodded, as best she could, but no more easily than it was to shake her head. Her eyes narrowed. Her eyes were screaming *'this is no time to play 20 questions you fool, my life is flashing before my eyes and I'm on my war years - so I've got about 10 seconds of oxygen left - get on with it!'*

Keith could hear footsteps.

'Good,' he thought, *'that's the driver coming to help, thank goodness, I'm getting nowhere fast with this old bird. The explanation had better be impressive.'*

CRACK!

Keith heard the ugly and frightening sound before he felt the searing pain in the back of his brain. Then Keith felt nothing.

The ambulance team found Keith first, lying astride the old lady who was now breathing normally but complaining bitterly about this 'bumbling buffoon' being on top of her. The Police arrived shortly afterwards in their Ford Focus.

'They should teach everyone proper first aid,' she screeched as they extricated Keith from his position. 'My throat is red roar because of this twit!'

Keith looked around the grey holding bay on the cruise liner. He was patiently waiting for the matron figure to return to him. The people around him had changed but the overall scene hadn't changed much. There were still a number of individuals and groups quietly languishing in the murk. All but one of the exiting clientele had gone down the brightly lit corridor which looked far cheerier than going off with the chap dressed all in black. This pleased and heartened Keith. The one who was due to disappear into the darkness with the moccasined chap, was a heavily tattooed man, complaining he shouldn't be there – he looked like he was winning his argument.

'Excuse me madam, I've been waiting here some time,' Keith said very politely.

'One moment Keith,' she replied, smiling kindly and returning behind her desk.

Keith stepped forward slightly to ensure they were still engaged.

The matron touched her display on 'A' and a list of names appeared. She typed in 'Armstrong' and she touched the letter 'K' and swiped her finger across the screen, moving the entries right to left. 'Keith T. Armstrong' appeared in front of her.

'Please can you confirm your date of birth?' she said looking up from the screen at Keith.

'8th June 1971.'

'You seem surprised at my system, were you expecting scrolls?' She scanned the screen and continued, 'ah, yes, the year of decimalisation. There were three Keith Armstrong's born on the 8th June 1971. One in the Philippines of mixed Philippine/English parentage – doesn't fit your profile I suppose, one in Scunthorpe born in an alley, but he has already been through and one in High Wycombe, born in a shrubbery; which is you,' she said buoyantly. 'I like that imagery – born in a shrubbery. I know it's a name and not a gardening feature, but all the same,' she said, wrinkling her nose up and enjoying a moment to herself. 'I'll update your records, but if you can stand over there by the door behind you, that will be fine.'

Keith obliged and stood next to the door indicated.

As matron touched the screen with a final flick of her hand, Keith was propelled back through the door into the corridor. His eyes remained focussed on matron and she seemed jolly pleased with the process - never breaking eye contact or her smile.

Keith's family were waiting for him in the outside corridor and they cuddled him closely.

Heggie sat in front of the row of his caged homing pigeons in shed number seven of his garden. He spoke to them in pigeon. He relayed a series of detailed instructions. He had the upmost confidence they could complete the task he was setting for them. Heggie Pump was a pioneer of the individual cage movement. Most of the other pigeon fanciers in England kept birds together in one large cage. Heggie's separated arrangement was the five star hotel equivalent. He was convinced his birds were the happiest on the continent. He lovingly took the bird from the cage displaying the name plate 'Marcus' and carefully attached a message to its leg. He whispered to it, kissed it on its crown and let it fly. He did the same with the birds in the cages marked 'Amelia' and 'Daphne'.

The cage marked 'Heggie' was the only one which remained occupied.

'Come on out old boy,' Heggie said to the bird in English. 'Now, the other birds know where they're going. They've been taught how to do it.

You, my champion, have an even stiffer task. You're not going to an address; you're going to find a person. Heggie attached a message to the leg of the bird and then reached inside the cage and retrieved the two photos that had been stuck to the side. 'This is a picture of the chap I need you to find,' showing the bird for the final time a picture of Fuzzy Cat, 'and this is where you will find him,' showing the bird a picture of a ford focus police car. Heggie wished the bird good luck in his native beak.

'Up you come Keith, up you come.'

Keith could hear a familiar voice in the distance and he felt he was being tugged towards it. Keith had been floating comfortably around, nice and warm with gentle, elevator type music playing in the background. Keith quite liked where he was but he forced himself to open his eyes. He could see two shadows standing over him. His eyes felt like stone; both gritty and heavy.

The shadows were watching him. *'Why are they watching me?'* thought Keith. *'Can't they see I'm awake? Can't they see my eyes are open? Have I got a bat in the cave and they're too polite to mention it?'*

It was Heggie who spoke first, Keith recognised the voice.

'You've been out for ages man!'

'Crikey, you must have played some heavy stuff, I can't even remember getting in the chair! Did we drink a lot? Katy's going to be annoyed. I didn't do anything embarrassing did I? Did I fall asleep? Aaghh, my head!' Keith's voice was slurred and he felt slow. This frightened him somewhat. Keith could feel he was in hospital; the bone dry, stiff sheets were a giveaway.

'You've been in an accident Keith and the Inspector here would like to ask you a couple of questions. I'll be right here though.'

The other shadow stepped nearer.

'Hi, you don't know me, but I'm from the Police and I need you to answer a few questions.'

'I do know you,' thought Keith *'you've been in my shed.'*

'Is this your wallet?' the Inspector said, lifting up a brown rectangle shaped thing.

Keith could hardly focus on it, not only because his eyes didn't feel like they were his, but also because the Inspector's arm which held the wallet aloft, kept jerking it out of focus each time Keith got a location on it; it was the chicken wing thing.

'Open it please,' Keith said huskily and in a way which surprised him because it sounded right out of the movies. He imagined himself as the key witness, balancing between life and death, injured in the bed and being questioned by the Police. The success of the whole investigation would hinge on what he said next.

'Yes, that's my 'Milkshakershake' loyalty card.' Keith thought that they would have to rewrite that part for the movie. 'Yes, that's a picture of my two children stood next to our Christmas tree and a phonics sticker of 'ee' and 'ier' that Carina stuck in there some time ago.'

'There was a car involved in your accident. Can you remember what colour it was?'

'Yes,' replied Keith and winced as the pain leapt up his back as he nodded.

'Don't over do it old chap. Stay as still as you can. What colour was the car?'

'Green, it was bright green, with flowers on the side. I've seen it a few times in the village; it is usually parked around the back of the Chequers pub next to the caravan in the car park.'

'Thanks – that's very helpful and all I need to know for now – you get some rest,' said the Inspector.

The Inspector turned to Heggie. 'You'd think people who commit these kind of crimes would at least try and keep a low profile - and not turn up in highly recognisable cars! I've got some investigations to make. I'll see you later.' The DI, now invigorated by the thrill of the chase, impressively rushed out of the ward.

'So what's happening Heggie, where's Katy?'

'Your wife's been here pretty much all the time, but she's popped back home to change and pick Ford and Carina up from school. You've been under for two days Keith, knocked out man. Laid there, just doing nothing – not even a flinch. I would like to think my little ensemble of tunes I played for you helped you re-surface. I started with some happy tracks sung by Dean Martin to ease you in softly, then onto the legend that is Bob Marley to put you into a good place. I then hit you with some Red Hot Chilli Peppers to liven you up – I'm sure your brain was bobbing to the mental guitar on 'Universally Speaking'. I lived it with you Keith - the split headphones enabled me to be right in there with you. I think what did it though, was my recording of the commentary from the Cheltenham Festival laid over Jim Morrison's 'American Prayer', I'm very pleased with that. Do you remember anything?'

'I do rather have the Chilli's in my head and could right fancy an afternoon at the races.'

'No, not the music man, although that is rather interesting, I mean about the accident?'

'Not much. Was I cycling up the hill?'

'That's right.'

'A driver was having a heart attack and then there was the old lady's mouth. Ugh, the old lady's mouth! Slobbery and wet, open and flapping like a rubbery carp, getting nearer and nearer.' Keith raised his hand and inspected his fingers.

'You were knocked off your bike. The Police think it was for your betting slip. Did you know you saved a little old lady's life, you hero?'

'Life saver 'eh? That's a first for me. My Mum will be very proud.'

'Yeah, man. The old lady was choking but you unblocked her when you fell on her.'

'She must have had rather a small set of dentures. I couldn't seem to find them if my memory serves me right.'

'They scanned you when you came in and they found a nasty black lump on the back of your head, underneath the tape on your helmet. The doctors feared the worst, that it was a colossal clot that needed surgery immediately. It turned out it was the old lady's boiled sweet, a black and white humbug I think – it got stuck in her throat and then stuck in your hair!'

Chapter 23

Public Investigations

The Police had been following up on their investigations regarding Heggie's broken greenhouse windows. Fuzzy Cat had attended the scene on a number of occasions. The suspicion was that he enjoyed the serenity of the garden and the opportunity to chill out in Keith's shed.

It was dusk on a Wednesday when Fuzzy Cat arrived again at Heggie's house. There were no lights on in the house so he crunched his way along the gravel of the side path and out onto the expanse of the show lawn nearest the house. The grass was finely trimmed and displayed succinct lines right up to the borders. The DI clocked that the rest of the garden was well established and the trees and shrubs provided a wall of shelter from the neighbouring properties. He was well surrounded and fairly secluded.

The DI surveyed the area again, wondering about the motive. His hunch was that this was not simply a case of kids smashing glass for kicks. Whoever did it was likely to have been in the garden at the time as they had used the laxton superbs from the locale as the projectiles. There were no other laxton superb trees within lobbing distance – he had checked all trees in the vicinity against the typical characteristics in his Usbourne book of British trees. The DI was always keen to learn new things; even though the force were keen to pasture him off as a stuck-in-his-ways officer. The local Co-operative didn't stock laxton superbs and the nearest stockists were in Uxbridge, a long distance in the apple carriage stakes.

The DI had a worrying doubt that the act could have been an effort to lure the inhabitants of the house outside to investigate. Although some distance from the house, the smashing glass would have been audible from the kitchen. Wealthy people, possibly with a past and or a connection to the big bands, could be the target of some kind of revenge or kidnap plot, or worse still – a misguided intrigue in those bands. This wasn't a common occurrence in Prestwood, but all the same, the DI considered it as a possibility – he read the press and the police bulletins and was always surprised what humankind could get up to or sink down to.

'When all possibilities have been disproven, whatever you're left with, however impossible, is the truth,' he misquoted to himself from the great detective Sherlock Homes. He kept this misquote close to him for unfathomable occasions such as this. It kept him focussed and gave him reassurance and strength.

There was a movement ahead of him - something travelling from the lilac bush in the direction of one of the fir trees. The DI focussed on the fir tree. He half wanted to identify the type of fir and he fingered his tree book in his DI style overcoat. It had been the slightest of movements but the DI saw it. He imprinted the form and the size on his mind, a mental photograph which he now recalled. He closed his eyes and studied the image. It was large...... male and...... well built. It didn't strike him as being Mr Pump but it was such a fleeting movement that he couldn't be sure. He tried to match his library image of Mr Pump against the new one. He ruled Mr Pump out.

He crept slowly and stealthily, as a DI should do, towards the fir tree. He opened his eyes wide and fixed them dead ahead so that he could cover

171

the range in front of him and his peripheral vision would spot any movement to the side. Instantly, he calculated the possible escape routes, the probability of being assaulted and the likelihood of a complaint against the Police for startling owners in their own gardens. It was a warm evening so people could be up to all sorts in the privacy of their shrubberies as the DI had discovered on numerous occasions.

He took a wide trajectory around the fir tree, as wide as the other trees would permit so no-one could jump out on him. He found nothing. He detected that someone had been there; the thin covering of grass in the shade of the tree was, in places, rising again after being suppressed. *'So why?'* he asked himself. *'What was this to do with Hector Pump the owner of the house? Was it a neighbour? Was this merely a route through to somewhere else? Were they hiding here from someone else?'*

'Hi DI' called out Heggie from behind him. The DI jumped out of his skin. He was so far into the crime scene that his usual sharp radar had not detected the approach of Heggie from behind him.

'Was that you I saw up here?' the DI asked, composing himself quickly and maintaining the air of a competent law enforcement officer. The public had to have confidence in their police force.

'I was taking some leisure time in my perennial border over there, not over here – I guess you wouldn't have seen me – I was well entrenched in the foliage.'

'Is that normal?'

'Probably not when you think about it.'

'No, I mean normal for you?'

'Well, yes. When I have the opportunity and it is fine weather, you could usually find me out here in one of my borders at this time of the evening.'

172

'Why would you say that someone should be in your garden?'

'I don't know – I've no enemies if that's what you mean. I generally keep myself to myself. Could it be a random weirdo perhaps?'

'They're the worst, unpredictable,' the DI mused, stroking his wiry moustache.

'What did they look like?' Heggie asked.

'Didn't get enough of a look. It was subtle and fast. Your ordinary policeman might not have seen it.'

'Creepy.'

'Creepy indeed for you. What with this and the less than accidental accident to the fella in the house at the end of your garden, it makes me wonder what on earth is happening here in Prestwood. I'll keep up the surveillance; you make sure you keep your windows and doors locked at all times and your pets indoors.'

'Okay man, I'll try and find my tortoise.'

Chapter 24

Private Investigations Part 1

A creeped out Heggie Pump ruminated on the recent events and called for Hubert Cheese.

Chapter 25

Private Investigations Part 2

A man stood in Heggie Pump's garden conversing with one of the trees. He was slight, short and wiry, with a wizened face. He looked like he could move as fast as a ferret if he needed to. A bobble hat sat slightly askew on his head, the side knit covering his ears and the tassels, ending in bobbles, rested unevenly on his shoulders. He was wearing a blue patterned shirt of good quality, red denim jeans and light Converse style pumps.

Heggie Pump watched him from the window of his shed. From what it looked like, the man was really questioning the tree - interrogating it almost.

'Cheese,' Heggie called out, 'it's great that you could come at such short notice. Come on over into the shed once you've finished with that apple tree.'

After a few moments, Cheese appeared at the shed door. 'I take it that is the tree from whence the apples were purloined.'

'How did you know?' Heggie asked.

'One of your wives told me. It willow not tell me anything though.'

'So, it walnut talk will it!'

'Fir all the questioning it stayed plane silent.'

'Oh, you're good at punning on tree names, I like that. Come and sit down – long time no see and you don't look a day alder.'

'Ooohhhh,' they both said at the same time as a result of Heggie's 'alder' pun.

Heggie invited Cheese to sit down, he wouldn't have otherwise.

'Really good of you to come and help me out with this mistree,' Heggie continued as they both sank into facing sofas. 'Will you stay a while? I'm shook up a bit and it would be good to have you at the elm of the investigations.'

'I'll certainly cedar what I can do - although it doesn't seem like a trip to the beech, with so little to go on as described in your pigeon note. I don't know how that pidge made it with such a large piece of correspondence.'

Heggie groaned at the continuous punning. 'Where would you like to stay – the guest bedroom is made up, or there is the turret for old time's sake? Your choice.'

'Down here in this shed will be the poplar choice, aspen too much time up on the turret anyway and I feel the damp in my bones more these days. Here will also be a good vantage point if anyone should come back.'

'It's noon, we should eat. I've packed us some ham baguettes,' Heggie said cheerily, content in the knowledge that ham baguettes were on the menu and that his old friend was on the case.

They talked through the events of the window smashing and the Police sighting in the garden. There wasn't much to go on indeed, but Cheese thought he would make a start right away, straight after lunch and a quick snooze. Cheese agreed to meet Heggie back at the shed at 9pm sharp, to update him on his investigations. After his nap, Cheese proceeded to The Green Man and stayed there all afternoon.

At 9pm, Cheese returned to the shed, eagerly waited for by Heggie.

'Well, how did you get on?' Heggie enquired.

'I established a first class intelligence gathering point and made some good progress,'

Cheese beamed. 'The good progress is that I've thought of a name for the case, "Lurkergate".'

'And, anything else?'

'Not really, it's early days yet.'

'Okay,' Heggie responded, rather flatly.

'I do have a theory though,' Cheese went on. 'The person we are looking for just might be female.'

'How do you deduce that Sherlock?'

'Think of a person well known for throwing things around? Have a guess.'

'Nope – nothing's coming to me,' pondered Heggie.

'Tessa Sanderson – she did it. Yep, she was always throwing things around.'

'Javelins mainly. But then so did Fatima Whitbread.'

'Oh, hadn't considered her,' Cheese said rather disappointedly that his theory had been so easily dispelled. 'Perhaps....' he went on, 'How about Tessa Sanderson AND Fatima Whitbread were both at it... having rekindled their old rivalry and seeing who could throw an apple the furthest when the accident happened.... or perhaps they were throwing apples at each other. I'm not sure how well they got on together, it's a good 'un.'

'But why my garden?'

'A ready source of apples,' Cheese offered.

'Not sure Cheese – it doesn't seem plausible. I don't think they live around here.'

'How about Phil Tuffnell? He was always throwing things around and he's a mischievous type. Does he live around here?'

'Nope. I'm not sure about the validity of your theorising.'

'I may know more tomorrow after I've studied the scene of the lurker. Now, I must get an early night, I'm exhausted from all this detective work. See you on the morrow.'

Cheese dedicated a good 30 minutes of his morning to studying the garden. He checked the size of any footprints he found and then measured his own shoe size to eliminate them from his list. He was left with nothing to go on so he returned to the shed for a long and inspiration inducing libation. At noon, he and Heggie lunched together on cheese baguettes.

'Is this Welsh cheese Heggie - and did you have to cut it Caerphilly?'

'Edam well isn't and, edam well was careful.'

The rest of the day, Cheese investigated the case from a new location, The Chequers, and he pondered all afternoon.

Back at HQ at 9pm sharp, the second day briefing was being delivered.

'No entry or exit footprints to speak of but grass which had been bent over temporarily – that's what the Police said, right?'

'Yep,' Heggie replied.

'I think we are looking at a local man. He came here in some sort of flying machine - hence no footprints.'

'Go on,' said Heggie, humouring him.

'I'm fairly sure in saying that it was the ex-Dr.Who and Timelord, Colin Baker. Now I know for a fact that HE lives locally to here in High Wycombe. How's that for a deduction?'

'It's a good one, rather than a good 'un, but he wouldn't necessarily have to live nearby if he had a Tardis, would he?'

'That's a good point and well made,' Cheese ruminated and there was a pause in discussions.

178

Heggie and Cheese looked out of the shed windows onto the garden.

'It seems a bit brighter in here today – have you cleaned the windows?' Heggie asked.

'Not I. I thought it was you being a good landlord.'

'Well I didn't either. That's peculiar. Why would someone want to clean all the windows of this shed? The girls are away at the moment and they wouldn't come up here anyway.'

'Perhaps they wiped off a bit to see in and then thought the only way for it not to be noticed is if they cleaned the whole lot.'

They sat in silence for a moment, thinking through possible explanations. Heggie's thought process was just reaching the chilling implications of the act when Cheese started up.

'Got it! It's that bloke with the small guitar. Not Norman Wisdom, the other one, ooh, George Formby. There's your man! He was always cleaning windows.'

'He's been dead a while I think,' chuckled Heggie.

Chapter 26

The Game's Afoot

'You're doing very well,' the nurse would say to Keith periodically as she passed the end of his bed. The meal time conversation followed a similar pattern. 'Egg or ham?' she asked, handing Keith an egg sandwich. 'It's not serious, but you will have to stay with us for a couple of weeks. Brown or white?' Keith looked at the sandwich already on his tray to see what he had chosen. 'You gave us a right scare.'

'You said that yesterday,' Keith thought, I'm not a goldfish.

'Cherry or vanilla?' Keith looked at the label on the yoghurt pot which had been placed on his tray. Cherry was leading 6 - 3. Tea, coffee or water?' Keith still hadn't said anything as he took his coffee. 'They do that with cranial impacts, that's a head injury to you Keith.' The nurse was even at it. 'Cheese and a cracker or just cheese?'

Heggie popped in every day. Keith was always pleased to see him. Although not particularly serious, Keith's injuries would keep him in hospital for two weeks - just enough time for his hair to start growing again where the humbug had been surgically removed.

'Keith.'

It gave Keith a start, he must have dozed off. Heggie tossed a grape he had brought for Keith up into the air and caught it in his mouth with a plop. He had been there for quite some time, sitting quietly, munching on the grapes and thinking all the while. Keith viewed the diminishing vine, by the time he would manage to move over to the side of the bed, there would be no grapes left for sure.

'Everyone loves the shed idea you know, as a kinda music listening studio. We want to set one up in the throbbing metropolis – that's London to you Keith.'

'I love it when you translate for me Heggie! You've obviously been translating a lot for me when I've been out cold – even the nurse is translating for me.'

'Nope,' replied Heggie, 'it just must be you.' Plop, the last grape disappeared.

'Is that you and Marcus?' Keith said through an aching jaw.

'Well actually, it's me, Marcus, Amelia and Fuzzy Cat. Amelia's been cut loose from GIZMO music and leaves in one week. She adamant it's because she's a girl. They've given her job to, as she puts it, a 'suitius-knobbus'. Apparently he knows now't about any of the business, but is a bit of a poster boy and has shiny shoes, patent I think they call it.' Heggie delicately unfurled the wrapper on a mint chocolate Viscount biscuit he had produced from his pocket.

'I'd bought these for you, but think it's a bit churlish now to give you only one as I ate the other four on the way. I'll get you another pack next time. And as for Fuzzy, he's being pushed out to pasture. His life's work gone, although I don't suppose he misses the quotas and targets. Both of them are hopping mad.' Heggie smoothed the last corner of the biscuit's foil in a show of solidarity sadness.

'Do you remember Keith, we had that conversation about being lost? Well, I think we have all sort of collectively come to that point, for different reasons, man, but essentially we want to give your thing a go. Are you in Keith?'

181

Keith lay in his bed. He thought about the wonderful opportunity for a good few minutes. Heggie rustled a solitary wine gum from the share sized bag he had just taken from his pocket. 'Sorry,' he said rather sheepishly, 'couldn't resist.'

Keith didn't really have to think about it too much. 'It's rather the opportunity I've been waiting for, to really work for myself rather than work for myself for someone else if you see what I mean and I do have some spare cash from my winnypoos. I think it's a goer but I'll ask Katy first, she's in later. How much are we looking at?'

'Exactly one thousand of your earth pounds.'

'A grand? Is that it? Are you and Marcus bankrolling this? It hardly seems fair me only putting a grand in and you soaking up the rest of the costs.'

'No, no. It's the five of us; we're all putting a grand in each.'

'Ha-ha! Five grand, that's hardly going to give you a big swanky joint up town is it! When was the last time you went to London Heggie? The prices have gone up a bit you know. You're as bad as my Dad; he still thinks that jeans only cost four pounds.'

'They still do, in some department stores,' Heggie said, straightening the outside hem of his jeans and admiringly smoothing down the fabric. 'We're going to use other people's money – we're gonna get us some investors.' Heggie slowed down on the word 'investors' and did his usual magic creating moment by raising his hand up from stroking his jeans across the air in front of him in an arc.

'I expect you're all well connected so this should be a cinch!'

'Wrong again dear boy, we're going to do this without utilising any of our contacts - for two reasons. Firstly, we don't want anyone to know it's us; they'll smell something's going on and start snouting around. We don't want to lose any advantage - on this one, the element of surprise is going to be key. Fuzzy is our front man, lead on the 'quelle buffoon unknown' role. He knows no-one and is playing it like he knows nothing about anything. Says his success is down to his years of police investigating and assuming different personas to crack the most unusual of crimes.'

Heggie paused for a moment, now having lost his train of thought. This was happening more frequently these days – he would find himself in a totally different thought area, thinking about the most unusual of things. 'Ah, that was it. I'm on the second of two points. And B, not using our contacts is filling the 'we've lost our way' bit. This is the thrill of the chase, the succeeding on one's own merits, bit. The focus, the drive, the plan, the direction, the motor, the motivation, the rekindling, the achievement, the horizon.'

'Crikey!' Keith mused, 'we've really lost our way.'

'Of course, we'll use all the contacts we have for the opening night! That's just good business. And now you must rest dear boy. We want to get going with the planning; can we use your shed?'

'Of course, I'll tell Katy when she comes in.'

'Good, that's agreed then.'

As Heggie hurried out, Keith spotted the new Asda value labels on the back of Heggie's jeans. *'That man,'* he thought, *'is comfortable with himself.'*

'Ah Heggie, I must have been dozing again, I didn't see you. How long have you been there?'

'About two minutes. Only enough to eat one of the Tunnock's wafer chocolate bars I brought you.'

Heggie held up a flattened wafer foil so Keith could see. 'Best treat in the world. I don't know how they make them so well balanced between chocolate, wafer and caramel. They sell 500,000 of these each day Keith. I've left you the other four.'

'How's the planning going?'

'Great, Fuzzy is in town looking at premises and he thinks he is onto something – seems very aroused about floor layouts and building footprints. Amelia is dealing with the marketing side of things; she has a real talent for that. It's all coming on jolly nice. We will need you there next week to help – when are you getting out?'

'Tuesday.'

'Well that's perfect. Next week is perfect for progressing things,' said Heggie, beaming across his face. 'Now, tell me about these characters you see on the train, they always amuse me.'

'Did you know I had a rival, Heggie?'

'A rival 'eh, ooh, that sounds interesting.' Heggie leant forward and teased another wafer bar from the packet. 'Tell me about this rival of which you speak!'

'Yep, a rival in the newspaper stakes. He sweeps through the carriages when the train has stopped in Marylebone, hoovering up the now gratis media left by the other passengers. The Times is the most coveted sweeperooney, unless, of course, there is a token or voucher in one of the other papers. You must understand that we can both afford a morning paper, but that's not the point – this is about pride on a micro level, being successful and undetected. Call it immature if you like but it amuses me. The trick is to sit near, not too close or too far away from, a commuter who you know leaves his paper at the other end of the journey. You can't sit too close - that would result in you being too confined in the sweep and being detected - you can't just pick up someone else's paper with them stood there – that's really an infringement of etiquette. If you lurk, you will be detected. The sweep needs to be loose. Similarly, being too far away also poses problems - a potential rival will beat you to it.

'Take for example Wednesday 3rd March. The Times were running an Olympic Games pull-out section. I knew it and my rival knew it, they had been advertising it for some time.

'As you know, I get on the train at Great Missenden. Great Missenden is predominantly The Daily Telegraph. The majority of The Times readers get on at Amersham. My rival boards at Chalfont and Latimer. This rather hands him the advantage as the good number of seats available means he can chose where he sits. All goods are of course on display. Well on that Wednesday, he made a colossal schoolboy error in his seating position by sitting too close to the carriage doors and next to the sleepy man - who is always last off the train. This meant that he was extremely likely to get caught and look like a complete pauper if he tried to make his way back up the carriage to get someone else's newspaper. Easy pickings for me as I swept down the carriage and took the prize; The Times - avec the special pull out section for the greatest sporting show on earth. He had to settle for a Mirror from the next compartment – no Olympic special for him!'

'Tell me again about that poor old economist and those two venture capitalist fellas,' said Heggie, unwrapping another chocolate wafer 'that's one of my favourites.'

'Ah yes! We are of course talking about Ferneaux Sidley-Smith and Damian Jones, sworn arch enemies in the venture capitalist arena in

185

London and as captains of their respective cricket teams in the Lee and Great Missenden. I'm afraid I don't know the name of the poor old economist so let's call him Fred. Damian Jones is winning this year I understand, both in terms of wickets and runs and returns for investors – I've listed those in order of importance. Sidley-Smith is hopping, hopping mad!

'Fred gets it most mornings, usually from Sidley-Smith who sidles up and ruthlessly pumps him for information on the economy. 'Any updates old chap?' Sidley-Smith will say, wobbling the bits of his neck which don't fit inside his shirt collar and hang down to the sides. Fred would wriggle on his bench uncomfortably at the series of pointed and short, direct questions from the bald-headed man stood in front of him with puke white cheeks. Some people just aren't cut out for quick fire questions – it's just not the way they work. I would imagine that Fred is one of these and needs time to be considered - you could see if from the way he clutches onto his Financial Times. He's not a 'leaver' Fred; he keeps hold of the newspaper at the end of his journey and probably reads it at lunchtime.

'Operations normal, carry on then,' Sidely would say as he concluded the exchange.

'It's quite comical to see Sidley-Smith avoid all contact with Jones. Sidley takes the front car and Jones the rear car. I'm told they work in the same office and use the same entrance and lift, but a well timed programme means they do not cross paths. Sidley-Smith takes lunch punctually between 1.35pm and 2.35pm after Jones has safely returned having lunched from 12.30pm to 1.30pm. They use the same restaurant for lunch and Sidley always asks what Jones has eaten.

'I must say that Jones appears to be a thoroughly decent chap. Sidley however is a bit pompous. I hear that he marginally retains his tenuous, self elected position as the squire of Great Missenden, half of which his father still owns. He thinks he cuts a dashing figure walking along the High Street, umbrella hanging on one forearm and yes, you guessed it, a Financial Times neatly folded under the other. Peculiarly, he wears a Humber. I think that more people should wear hats, but I'm not so sure about Sidley's choice. My bus companion tells me that he used to wear pin stripes as a young man when sorting the finances of the nation. Now that he is more mature, he wears tweed suits and lightly checked shirts, dons facial hair and relies on his tailor to hide his growing midriff.

'I sat next to him once, which seemed to cause him unnecessary discomfort and annoyance, enough for him to crumple his neckerchief. Listens to Barry Manilow you know, although I will say that in my humble opinion, 'Cococabana' is one of the finest tracks you will find – it has the passion, the excitement and the raunchiness. So, okay, it's also my Grandma's favourite along with the 'Bermuda Triangle' and 'One Voice' but I think it is all acceptable stuff to be listening to on the train. Sidley however, is clearly embarrassed about the whole 'Barry' thing and takes great pains to hide the screen when he is selecting his morning's music on his MP3 player.'

'People are funny,' Heggie mused.

'You pick up a lot of body language signals just watching people. Some are very subtle - like turning the pages of a newspaper to infringe other people's personal space, nasty on a small scale but nasty nevertheless. Some are very unsubtle such as men sitting with their legs wide apart like some baboon, with one cheek slightly over the dividing line in order to secure the all important double seat.'

'It's good to see you on the mend Keith and back in good humour. You've given me a good idea. I'll see you tomorrow; I've got some final planning to do. I'll leave you the details of the arrangements for tomorrow in the usual place,' and he was gone again, with a flash of unbranded jeans.

Keith was back at home and doing his circular check of the garden. Heggie had clearly spoken to Katy as she was fine with Keith going into London the day after his release from hospital. There was a note on the shed, as arranged.

'Meet me at Great Missenden train station tomorrow, Wednesday. We will catch the first train after 10.30am (off peak so it's slightly cheaper).'

A gooey Amelia sat on a tall stool inside the Great Missenden Bookmakers. She had been there for 20 minutes or so since opening. There had been no other customers, so she had the freedom of the cards to pick her winners and to chat to the handsome one, as she saw it, of the ever-so slightly dangerous brothers who owned the establishment.

She ran her finger down the list of runners in the 5.45 at Kempton. Just the kind or race she liked, enough runners to get the place paid out to third, all lower grade in Class 6 and lightly raced so something could spring a surprise. These were important components when Amelia was picking the horses that would bring her the big pay-off. She started first, as usual, with the bottom weight horse. If it stood a chance and was a nice price she might look no further. If that didn't give her a selection, she would then check the top rated horse and compare this with the price - if it was one of the top four favourites she would ignore it. The process continued. If no horse in the race had won at all, she would select an un-raced horse. Only if this all had failed would she start to look at the detailed form and check for changes in running distances, drop in class or a change of stable. All the clues were there in the text in front of her but she liked her system best.

Amelia made her sixth selection. She completed the last line on her 'Lucky 63' betting slip, added the stake and ticked the each-way box which made it a lucky 126. She handed it to her handsome teller along with her £2.52 for the 2p stake she had chosen.

'Bookies delight!' the brother said.

'It'll pay thousands,' Amelia replied.

'Yeah, but one horse goes down and you've lost half your bets! Good luck though.'

'It's quiet in here – is business good?'

'It usually picks up about now with the pensioner rush.'

The door opened and in walked an older gentleman, tall and well built. The long overcoat did nothing to hide his well-worked on arms and shoulders. The thick veins running around the side of his bald head told you he was fit as a fiddle, not an ounce of excess fat.

Amelia sat at the desk, hands under her chin and tried to commandeer the Robinson brother's time.

'So apart from serving 'super-grampy' over there, have you got time to take me out for a coffee?'

189

'No, but do you need running up the hill again?'

'Not today, I've just come from a friends up the hill. Used to be in the music industry, like I am. You'll probably know him – he must be a local legend.'

The older gentlemen subtly moved position and studied the Kempton Park race card closer to where Amelia was.

'Come to the comfy seats, I'll get you that coffee,' said the owner, 'I'd like to hear more.'

Sat with her coffee, the owner gave Amelia more of his attention. The old boy was now settled with the Racing Post.

'Big business deal, somewhere near Trafalgar Square. That's all I can tell you. But after we have pulled it off, you can buy me dinner and I'll tell you all about it,' said Amelia, trying to impress.

'Who's the we? A bright girl like you could probably pull off any deal that you wanted.'

'I probably shouldn't say, but I think I can trust you! You don't know anyone in the music business do you?'

'We dabble in the nightclub business, we've an all-night rave just finishing up the road, right at this minute, but it's not the kind of music business you're talking about. All I know is horses and this place – and that I'm going to be taking a very successful and attractive lady out for dinner sometime soon.'

'Well, okay then.' Amelia giggled, now complete putty in her target's hand. 'We've got the music legend I told you about, a guy called Marcus who's the money man, the local retiring Police Officer for logistics and me of course – the front of house.'

The buzzer on the door sounded as the older gentleman left the shop. A large flat bed builder's van pulled into the bookies car park but the builders stayed inside the cab. Amelia looked at her watch.

'I've got to meet my colleagues, I've got to go,' she said and rushed out of the door, calling behind her 'see you soon for dinner, I'll pop back in to pick up my winnings and we can arrange a time then!'

Robinson brother number one heard the back door open and close as someone came in. He called through to his sibling.

'Cover the counter would you? I've got to go and see some commuters.'

'Do you really have to go now? I'm trying to find out which copper stole all our music equipment this morning. We've got egg on our face as well as 150 disgruntled ravers.'

'How did you let that happen? You can find out from in here – there's no-one about. Where are the keys to the hire car?'

'I left them on the counter, next to the till.'

The older gentleman took off his coat and climbed into the car parked outside the bookmakers. He reached a muscular tattooed arm across the car and opened up the glove box. He located Gatwick on the courtesy map and started the engine. 'I love the smell of these English hire cars,' he said as he slid the car into first gear.

A police car coming the other way pulled up alongside him. A policeman with a moustache and a flinch peered in through the window.

'Nasty tic you got there,' said the man in the hire car.

'Less of it. I can get rid of this tic – but you can't grow your ear back – on your way,' and he waved the driver of the police car on.

The tattooed man saw the Police pull up outside the bookmakers. The Robinson brothers came running out into the road looking for their car – only to see it disappearing into the distance.... not before, that was, the tattooed man saw them being arrested by the policeman who had just given him the once over.

'My last day on the job and I get to arrest you two, it just couldn't get any better,' Fuzzy Cat chirped.

'I want to make a complaint – one of your lot stole all of our music equipment last night and now this – this is Police harassment,' Robinson brother number one said.

'Shut it. Into the car with them lads and take them to Amersham police station, not Wycombe. You can drop me off at Amersham tube station on the way,' Fuzzy ordered.

Robinson brother number two was very irate. 'Too important are you now to even nick us? Something better to do up in London have you.......?' Robinson brother number one gave his sibling a sign and he fell silent.

Chapter 27

'A Travelcard Please, We're Off to London'

'Morning Keith.' Heggie was already at the train station. 'Shall we get a coffee?'

Lesley poured Keith a small coffee as he entered the kiosk and before he asked for it; he was good at remembering what people wanted. Heggie was impressed. Lesley was the lady who looked after all the commuters. She must have known nearly everyone who travelled, the trains they usually caught and their likely order for tea or coffee.

'It's busy in here – the coffee must be good,' Heggie said to Lesley by way of a compliment.

'The coffee's lousy – as you're just about to find out. It's busy 'cos they've had one of those illegal rave things in the old BT building last night and people haven't quite made their way back into London. Been hanging around here all morning making a nuisance of themselves to people like you.'

'I'll have a large lousy coffee then please, with milk,' Heggie said.

'Milk's over there love. Help yourself.' Lesley said in a helpful manner.

'Are you fit?' Heggie asked Keith when they were back on the platform, having made their coffee even colder with the cold milk.

'Ready and raring to go,' Keith replied and pretended to box Heggie with a few low mock blows to the stomach and a shimmying of the feet, 'what is it that you want me to do?'

'I'll reveal all as we go along but, for now, just be your usual very good company.'

Keith was generally good company, master of the small talk. He could see fun in most things and was generally an affable sort. He could do affable and good company rather well.

The train rocked and rolled steadily through the Chiltern countryside like a half awake snake; making its way lethargically to a sunny patch. It slid silently and slowly past the fields and the trees and the tube stations dotted along its route.

Keith returned from the toilet to find Heggie had moved location in the carriage and was discussing earphones with a group of lads who had got on at Rickmansworth.

'I've got the latest Sennheiser's CXC700 headphones with the three noise cancelling settings to match my varying aural environments, one for trains, a mid frequency for planes and a high pitched one for crowd noise. And if I flick this switch, it gives you the follow through function with the built in mic so I can hear people without taking off my earphones. How about that!'

Keith continued to his seat in the next bay of six – those lads must think he is a 'rediculant'.

'How much?' one of the lads asked.

'About £200. But get this... AKG have just launched their K3003 hand-made, brushed steel, crafted from one piece of metal headphones. It's got an equivalent power to two 16GB i-pads and they are the smallest three way earphones – similar to being front and centre, if you excuse the analogy.' A couple of the group sniggered but Keith didn't understand. 'Retail price of £1,000.'

'You've got to be seriously mental to buy a pair of them,' one of the lads said but then immediately looked at Heggie thinking that this crazy looking dude who is so into his music might just be seriously mental enough to buy them.

'Well, the tangle resistant cables nearly made me part with my reddies!' Heggie said as he got up and left the group.

Heggie rejoined Keith and the lads went on talking noisily. At Harrow-on-the-Hill, the carriage doors opened and in walked a rather peculiar gent with a strange hat that had two pompoms dangling down. Keith watched his progress. Keith found it hard to handle chaotic eccentrics and this one fitted the bill. Keith mentally urged him... *'go into the other carriage, there's plenty of room in there. Gooo on.'*

The chaotic eccentric turned right towards Keith and Heggie rather than left to the other carriage. Keith shifted in his seat. *'He'll surely take the clear four.'* The chap continued to walk on down the carriage. *'Keep it moving,'* Keith thought, *'right on down and through the doors to the next carriage. Why do people do that?'*

He sat opposite Keith and Heggie.

'Please don't talk to him Heggie,' Keith thought.

'Had a good morning?' Heggie asked the hat.

'Fruitful,' the Hat replied.

'Fruitful, 'eh! Well I would find it very ap-peal-ing if you would tell me about it, but make it pithy so I don't get the pip.'

Keith sunk at least four foot into his Chiltern Railways standard class seat.

The Hat opened his broadsheet newspaper and held it up between himself and Heggie so they couldn't see each other. Keith, occupying the window seat, could see both sides of the paper. The two men sat staring at each other as if the paper wasn't there.

The Hat was thinking hard and suddenly scrunched the paper down into his lap and said, 'if

195

I told you, try not to let it make you feel melon-choly.'

'What's this!' Keith thought, *'punning?'*

'Please do tell me, you've raisin my expectations. Kumquat have you found?'

Keith rolled his eyes and sank further back in his chair. *'This guy's clearly deranged but yet Heggie humours him.'*

The broadsheet shot up again. The Hat thought again, hard. The Hat lowered his paper to his lap having failed to find a fruit related retort so he delivered the statement: 'I've been investigating this case for a while now and a number of people have been implicated. We know certain sportsmen and women have a tendency to throw things around. In their profession, they can get a little boisterous and, things can get out of control. That may or may not account for the broken windows.'

'What on earth is he going on about?' thought Keith.

'I've pretty much excluded Colin Baker from my suspect list....'

'Good grief, random or what, he could attack us at any minute. Broken glass, sportsmen and Colin Baker?'

'... but I think the person in the garden is linked to acting or the entertainment business, a magician perhaps - to effect such a manoeuvre as disappearing from in front of the police like that. I would suspect the person we are looking for holds an equity card. I'm two steps away from proving a politician cleaned the shed windows.....'

Keith's mind entered overdrive, *'politicians cleaning shed windows?'* Keith was eyeing the route he needed to take to get to the alarm in case of an emergency.

'......they're always interfering, often to no benefit and we know some of them are up to no good. The surrounding area appears to be awash with politicians and Chequers is but an apple's throw from where you live Heggie.'

'He used his name... he called him Heggie!' In relief, Keith bolted up in his seat. 'Ha ha, ah! So you know each other, that's great..., I mean, that's good...... it's nice to meet up with friends...,' blurted a pleased Keith.

'Keith, this is Cheese. Cheese, this is Keith.'

The Hat nodded at Keith and continued. 'So, where does this leave us?' now addressing both of them. 'What links all of the above people?' Cheese paused and pondered. For dramatic effect, he brought his hands up in front of his face, fingertips touching. 'I think it goes right to the top! I suspect the Queen is behind it. They're in some kind of syndicate – watch out lads – you're on her turf today.'

'And on that bombshell, I'm off to the dunny,' sighed Heggie and he rose and left the carriage in search of the smallest seat on the train.

Cheese and Keith sat in an awkward silence as the train glided on.

At Neasden Junction the tracks multiplied and were filled with tube trains, busying themselves between the multitude of underground stops, noisy and a nuisance. They were showing off again to the diesel locomotives with flashes from the metal tracks interacting with the electricity power. The old snake though kept its composure and went about its business calmly.

'Are you coming with us today?' Keith asked Cheese after about 50 clickity-clacks of the wheels against the gaps between track lengths to get the conversation flowing again. 'I thought you might know what was going on; Heggie's been very secretive.'

'I would have loved to – it all sounds exciting but I'm off to Gatwick.'

'Travelling somewhere nice?'

'No. Just people watching – you never know who's going to show up or who will be meeting them. I'm off to Gatwick to follow up a lead.'

Keith was still confused. Confused by everything about Cheese and what was going on. He didn't push for anymore answers. Heggie would be back in a moment and the natural conversation would hopefully reveal more. *'Oh my, what's he doing now... he's shifting across towards me....why is his face changing and his eyes fixing on me...'*

'It's hard work being an eccentric Keith. It's a real life choice. Many people would be larger than themselves, but society doesn't permit. I've enjoyed it over these past weeks; I think I will keep it up. Look around you Keith – how many people are eccentrics and are they for real or normal? Is it a choice or an affliction? I think Keith, you've portfolloed some of you up there in your brain-box. You should let your magazma out more often.'

Keith thought he was right. He had given way to and given away some of his magazma. Partly through duty perhaps and partly for other reasons he couldn't quite bring to mind. His thought train was stopped as Cheese continued.

'Anyway for now, the person lurking may be interested in both of you. I've listened to people in the village. It's all there if you watch and listen. The lurker came through your garden Keith. They had plenty of opportunities to strike at either you or Heggie if they wished – but they didn't. Why was that? Definitely a lurker, but a lurker with a reason. Why have they been watching you both?

198

What's your connection? Is there one? I didn't want to worry Heggie so hence the pretence. Watch out today, both of you. I'm going to try and find out what's going on.'

Heggie rejoined them in the carriage and nothing further was said about Cheese's warning. Following the very sedate run in from Harrow-on-the-Hill, past the new Wembley stadium, the skip yard with its huge pile of rubble and the row of terraced houses where you could just get a glimpse of the vast variety of lives within half a mile or so, the three of them arrived at Marylebone Station, platform 2.

'The concourses are a lot quieter at this time of the day,' chirped Keith, enjoying the space and the freedom from the carriage. 'I usually compete in the 100 yard commuter dash to the ticket barrier of a morning. You could get trampled in one of those competitions, especially on platforms 1 and 2 as the barriers are in sight of where the train stops. Your professional barrier running days could be ended in a flash by the stern looking executive lady with the unfeasibly short skirt and slim-line Samsonite briefcase who gets on at Harrow-on-the-Hill. It's a world of difference travelling at this time Heggie. If one travelled on the later trains where one would get a window or, better still, a window and a double seat, one may feel that this is a very nice way to travel. But if you went earlier, where you may have to stand or be pinned in your chair by the very large, energy drink guzzling, chap who gets on at Chorleywood, you may think differently.'

'We're heading for Canary Wharf for a bite to eat,' Heggie said excitedly, 'it's a long time since I've been to Canary Wharf. In the old days Keith, it was easy to set things up – my word is my bond and all that. Then the money men moved into the industry and then into Canary Wharf shortly after it was redeveloped. Suddenly, the commercialers had gotten a hold and you had to present business cases, project tradjects, in-turns and out-turns and things. It became like you had to dance the monkey dance to get anywhere, begging almost, guarantees, paperwork, cash investment returns, merchandising percentages, contracts and the like. Gone were the days of trust when a deal could be put together over a handshake and a beer. I found I had to convince the PR people that it was a good investment and I'll get outcomes if I wanted to invite any contacts out for a short shift session with the top shelf when developing a deal.

'Were going to try that restaurant Keith, you know, the one you told me about where Sidley-Smith and Jones lunch; it must be good if they go there every day. My information tells me Jones is meeting a high profile Premiership footballer who wants to invest some of his mega earnings into a company for five to ten years, sort of a tax offset but with the potential for returns.'

They bade farewell to Cheese who went down into the underground at Marylebone and they walked to Baker Street, much the same route Keith did most mornings. Keith entertained Heggie with stories of the eccentric things he had seen on the underground. Heggie, as always, was entertained.

'Do you think Cheese is an eccentric or do you think he's just putting it on?' Keith asked Heggie.

'He's putting it on. I think he's worried about the goings on but doesn't want to worry me unnecessarily – he's covering it up with that tomfoolery. I've known him for many years and I can read him quite well.'

To change the subject, Heggie suggest they spot more 'rediculants' on their journey.

They traversed the two escalators down into the depths of Baker Street with its wall tile designs of the silhouette of Sherlock Homes and the various posters depicting Sidney Paget illustrations of scenes from the Arthur Conan Doyle books.

'Ah, Sidney Paget, Keith,' Heggie said rubbing his handsome chin, 'no one knows who he is really. They probably think Conan Doyle did the drawings. You sometimes need a lucky break Keith. The publishers accidentally sent him the letter of commission rather than his younger brother, Walter Paget, and he ended up illustrating a series of twelve short stories that ran from July 1891 through December 1892. The illustrations gained a darker tone as Paget used the black-and-white medium to reflect the grim mood of the stories. The deep, shadowy look of Paget's illustrations was a probable influence on American detective movies as well as film noir and has had a profound influence on every film version of the Holmes stories.

'Paget gave the instantly recognizable deerstalker cap and Inverness cape to Holmes, details that were never mentioned in Conan Doyle's writing. The cap and coat first appear in an illustration for "The Boscombe Valley Mystery" in 1891 and reappear in "The Adventure of Silver Blaze" in 1893. The curved pipe was added by the stage actor William Gillette. Funny how the initial idea gets embellished and becomes more recognizable than the original. 'Yeah, I know that guy – the hat, the pipe and the cloak' – nothing of the sort. I wonder how the author felt about it.'

The platform announcer announced the platform number. His noise was largely ignored.

Platform directions didn't really matter to the majority of underground users, only the colour and direction is needed.

Having alighted at Canary Wharf after eight tube station stops, they agreed that three qualifying 'ridiculants' had been spotted.

In third place it was the Personal Assistant; carrying 72 Krispy doughnuts split into six boxes of twelve, all piled high and wide enough to be very unmanageable for one so small, even with soft un-heeled shoes.

Runner up was the eccentric old lady, sat on a station bench on the mezzanine level at Baker Street station, laughing insanely to herself with her legs wide enough apart (modesty in-tact thank goodness) to qualify her as a stout farmer's wife.

The winner, they both agreed, by a clear urban mile was the man dressed like the Joker out of the Batman comics with white paint he had put on the front centre part of his black shoes, drunk, and randomly abusing people in the carriage Keith and Heggie travelled in. He stood, gripping onto one of the upright poles, swinging and lurching as the carriage rocked. He picked on people, generally the ones who ignored him, shouting that it was his intention to liven things up. He did do, to a certain extent, but nobody could really hear what he was saying – he was a victim of the noise from the air conditioning and the roar of the machinery as it powered through a small tunnel and, because he was slurring so much. Heggie and Keith were not sure if he was coming home from somewhere drunk or he was just always drunk in the mornings.

To add to their haul of rediculants, they had the bonus of a famous person, albeit Colin Jackson, the former hurdler and now TV pundit, spotted on the escalator at Baker Street. Nice suit, well turned out, looked a million dollars.

They rose gradually and somewhat regally over two escalator rides and reached the mezzanine level of Canary Wharf. Here, somewhere between the Underground and 'street level' is a whole mini village.

'It's been a while since I've been here but I remember you can get pretty much all the basics to support the executive at work and the executive at home,' said Heggie.

'I've not been here before,' admitted Keith.

'People think this is a new concept, but when you think about it the same services are delivered from here as they were in the first days of the city – cobblers, locksmiths, eating and drinking establishments, banking and soliciting – both varieties. Here as well you can get artisan dough kneaded and your back muscles kneaded - for about the same price!'

Keith felt it was rather clinical and soulless, despite the attempt to be 'boutique-y'.

'I can see you're not buying it Keith. Canary Wharf itself takes its name from the number 32 berth of the West Wood Quay of the import dock. People often refer to that building,' Heggie said pointing to the tallest building, 'as Canary Wharf when in fact it is One Canada Square. I like it in life when you get those kinda misconceptions. It was the tallest building in the country for twenty years, all 50 storeys of the chunk. The original plans for a business district on Canary Wharf came from a guy called G Ware Travelstead but he was unable to find the money for his project, so he sold the plans to Olympia & York in 1987. Docklands Square, where they grouped the three towers was renamed Winston Square before being renamed as Canada Square. That building,'

203

said Heggie pointing to the same building he had done before, 'was called DS7 on the plans. You know how I know all this Keith? I know the guy who supplied all 500,000 bolts used during construction.

'Around 105,000 people work in Canary Wharfland. What do you think these companies do Keith?' Clifford Chance, Infosys, Fitch Ratings, Skadden, State Street and Thomson Reuters.'

Heggie paused for the answer whilst Keith pondered. 'They sound like pawnbrokers.'

'Close. This is home to the headquarters of numerous major banks, professional services firms and media organisations. In the late 1500's, the Port of London was alive with activity, trade was expanding and Docklands became a point of departure for merchant ventures - in 1620 the Mayflower set sail from Rotherhithe to America. Now the old Wharfkingdom boasts an international airport. You can get to over 30 destinations including Chambery and Zurich if you fancy a spot of skiing, Barcelona if you want to get yourself some sun and Florence if you want to get cultured up.'

They made their way across the expanse of the plazas. The bright sunshine and light breeze was a welcome change from the heat and humidity of the Jubilee Line. They strolled on, enjoying the sound of the fountain and the bustle of the early lunching executive ladies, trim and finely turned out.

Chapter 28

Operation 'The Fat King Music Listening Studio' Phase 1
The Restaurant

'Here's the restaurant Keith,' said Heggie pointing to a smallish unit with large glass windows and a French feel to the exterior decor. It looked to be pitched mid-range, slightly classy but affordable to entice the regular.

'Jones and Usavio, he's a goal keeper Keith, should be at Jones' usual table, the booth over in the corner. I've booked a table so we can watch. After you Keith,' and Heggie held the door open enabling Keith to enter the restaurant and proceed to the area to wait to be seated.

'Have you a reservation?' the maitre D' asked from somewhere under his long nose. He certainly looked the part, not that Keith had world knowledge in the subject of maitre Ds. He was tall, thin and elegant looking and he seemed to be able to glide towards them without moving his legs or ruffling any of the table cloths between the closely situated tables.

'Yes,' Heggie responded, 'for two please, under the name of Hucker, first name Ewold.'

The maitre D nodded and used the internationally recognised restaurant action for them to attend with him by bowing slightly and turning away. 'This way please Ewold Hucker and guest, I have arranged the table you desired,' and he glided again effortlessly before them.

'I think he got it Keith, he-he, but he's not rising to my puerility,' Heggie said delightedly looking back over his shoulder as he weaved between the tables, ruffling the tablecloths and brushing against some of the diners.

'Got what?'

'My little joke, the name I booked in.' Heggie paused. 'Don't worry dear boy, if it needs explaining.....'

'Do you think he has wheels on his shoes Heggie? Like the ones that you see kids wearing in shopping malls, wheelies I think they call them. They come towards you at a rapid pace and you don't know if they are in control or not and are going to knock you over and then, at the last minute, they veer away from you.'

'You can't get them in Brogues, I've tried.'

They settled into their seats at the table. Keith had spotted Jones and was watching him intently.

'It's rude to stare Keith, don't frighten the horses.'

'Drinks to start, sirs?' the maitre D asked, now the two of them had been given a moment to settle but not a moment to read the drinks menu. Lunchtime dining depended on promptness.

'A bottle of your house red for starters and a bottle of water please,' said Heggie.

'Lightly sparkling or still, Mr Ewold Hucker?'

'Ooh, yes, fizzy please.'

'And Mr Hucker's guest?'

'The same please, lightly sparkling would be fine.'

Keith wondered why he wasn't as comfortable as Heggie using the word 'fizzy' in a standard London eatery, at lunchtime, a million miles from his house, that he was unlikely to frequent again, booked by someone else using an alias.

'He's definitely got it, otherwise he wouldn't be using my full name. Ha!' Heggie settled himself and appeared professional. Keith was none the wiser and continued to wonder what Heggie was going on about. 'You of course know Jones, Keith, you described so very well that when I came in to book this table, I spotted him straight away. I agree Keith, his suits are exquisite and tailored extremely well. Never wears a tie you said and favours the open necked stripy shirt look. Recognised him in an instance. Works very well on him in my opinion. I respect a man who follows his own path in the face of convention. That Keith Richards is another one, he's led his life on his terms, I think that Jones is doing the same within his sphere and I like that.'

In Keith's head a little capsule broke and the fluid of realisation poured out. It was warm and it trickled outwards over all the bumps and into the cavity of his brain. He thought to himself - *'that's it! I'm not comfortable with myself. Heggie is comfortable wearing jeans from ASDA and ordering 'fizzy' water. Jones wears his shirts open at the neck. They have the guts, no, the magazma to do it. I need to find my magazma!'*

'You seem to be very well informed Heggie, getting this table and knowing what Jones is up to and at what time,' said Keith rather admiringly of the man who laid in his borders and dedicatedly engaged in rural pursuits such as apple growing. 'This table does indeed provide a rather good vantage point of the proceedings.'

They perused the menus. A waiter appeared as if from nowhere.

'There's a good selection,' Keith said, 'are we having starters?'

'Have what you want.'

'That really doesn't help me make a decision. If I have a starter and he doesn't, it makes me look like a fat pig. If I don't order one and he does, then I'll have missed out on one where I wanted

one. Be comfortable Keith,' he told himself, *'set your own stall out'.*

'I think I'll have the bruchetta and a side of olives to start, followed by the lime and coriander chicken.' The starter was a result of his new found magazma and side of olives was a direct result of what the Hat had said on the way in on the train.

'Me too,' Heggie said to the waiter, folding his menu straight up.

'Not bad!' thought Keith, pleased.

They sampled the house red with great gusto.

'Planning Keith, it's all in the planning and thanks to your stories from the trains, we got the lead-in we required. These olives are really rather good aren't they.'

'Good, I'm pleased you approve.' Keith's magazma battery increased with energy at the approval of the olives.

They both watched the bustle of the restaurant. Keith, given his process improvement mind, charted the operational workings of the restaurant and its staff. He thought they ran a tight ship, but they could have improved on the hand off between mains and desserts.

Heggie watched the people. There were loners and groups. Same sex tables and mixed. Clusters of suits and clusters of professionals who didn't need to dress in suits. There were tables of young executive types who were bullishly reliving their exploits. They had done this to that person and managed to pull off the most amazing deals. There were tables of the older executives who were cagey about their exploits as they knew too well that any slip in information gave advantage to others, and anyway, they had nothing to prove these days – they were probably top of the tree. There were tables of the younger crowd – mainly

208

in HR and admin who complained and told stories about the ignorant suits and bitched about alpha females.

'The time now is 1.20pm,' said Heggie, spinning the outer dial on his watch around. 'In approximately five minutes, Jones will take Usavio back to the office to complete the investment deal. This chicken is rather good as well.'

As Keith had his back slightly to the area Jones was sat in, Heggie began to give a running commentary so he didn't need to turn around. 'It's 1.25pm Keith and Jones has signalled to the waiter he wishes to pay the bill. There is something delicious in this sauce that I can't quite put my finger on; I will have to ask for the recipe. I expect Sidley will be leaving his desk about now, according to the intelligence that you've provided. He's probably placing his pen back in its box on his desk and tucking it neatly back into his well ordered drawer.'

Keith was considering how much to charge his magazma battery with the reference to 'intelligence gathering' and 'this chicken is good'.

'Excuse!' Heggie bellowed, waving at the waiter.

Keith jolted in his chair with surprise and missed his mouth with his fork laden with coriander chicken, tasty sauce and the last bits of the garnish. A salad leaf stuck to his chin and pointed downwards as if it were a slim, green Chinese beard.

'Sorry Keith, I had to delay Jones by a few minutes so I needed to divert the maitre D to us first. Thought speaking in French would do the trick.'

'Oui?' the maitre D enquired.

'Oh, you're good!' Heggie said, impressed at the speed in which he arrived. 'What's the cheesecake special today?' asked Heggie.

'Raspberry and citrus.'

'Tres bon, we'll have two when you are ready and ...'

'It's the pickled 'Moulin a la poivre cinq' you're wondering about sir which makes the sauce so special,' and turning to Keith he continued 'that's the five mixed pepper corns which have been grown and pickled 'dans le Francais' for a fuller and hotter flavour, sir.' Keith's magazma battery leaked a little.

The maitre D, clipped his heels, dipped his head and shoulders ever-so slightly towards the two of them, and left the table.

Heggie turned to Keith. 'On table 21, over in the corner to your left Keith...' Heggie paused to allow Keith to turn a little. 'That's it, near the dessert trolley.... you may recognise a familiar face.'

'Ah! It's Marcus,' Keith said in realisation, 'doesn't he just look dapper! What a coincident. I'll call him over, he might as well join us.'

Keith started to rise in his chair.

'No, Keith. Sit down dear boy. You're not getting this!'

Keith shot back down.

'We're undercover Keith, incogni-visible. That's two words joined together Keith, incognito and invisible – did you see what I've done there. We're both words at the same time me and you Keith, at this minute and on this mission.'

'Okay, I'm not really getting this but I'll try harder,' Keith replied, a little disappointed with his lack of where-with-all.

'Marcus has sponsored Usavio's football kit. It's just a small investment, all clubs do it to raise sponsorship money and although you don't get any free tickets or anything, you do get to meet the footballer, which happened last week.'

Heggie loaded his fork with the last of his lime and coriander chicken which provided an opportunity for Keith to take a sip of his red wine.

'Now Marcus!' Heggie blurted not all that quietly; urging Marcus into action. The blurt meant that Keith had a near miss when sampling his wine.

Across the restaurant, Marcus rose from his seat and intercepted Jones and Usavio in the reception area.

'That's great – Usavio remembers Marcus from the other day.' The group stood exchanging pleasantries, with Marcus going for the world record in the longest handshake ever with Usavio.

'That's good Marcus,' Heggie continued, 'keep it going; but don't crush his hand too much, he needs it on Saturday! Come on, come on, where is Sidley?' Heggie was feeling for his wine glass without looking as he surveyed the plaza for Sidley, which made it difficult for Keith who was in the process of topping him up. Keith took a sip of his wine – using both hands now to hold the glass as he wasn't sure what to expect next.

'This is exciting stuff Heggie, a meal and a show – with commentary!'

'Here comes Sidley!' exclaimed Heggie, now excited. Keith was ready this time and he had his glass well away from his lips.

Heggie was excited. Keith admired his excitement. 'Excited' was the second of the three words that he would use to describe Heggie. He was excited about life. It didn't particularly matter what was going on, he was excited about it. He was the kinda guy who would get to a theme park early in order to queue and soak up the

211

atmosphere. He would get to a theme park early so he could listen to the band who played to entertain the guests as they queued. He would be excited about preparing to go to that theme park from the moment he work up early; even if this meant him not preparing for the day properly. He would be excited the night before.

'I can hardly keep up,' Keith said through a mouthful of raspberry and citrus cheesecake which had been delivered in the intervening moments, 'and the pud is just wonderful, well worth the cost, especially at London prices.'

'I rate any restaurant that prides itself on cheesecake. When I came in here last week, the manager told me he'd reduced the price of the cheesecake so that more people had it – 'an education programme,' he referred to it as.'

A rather hungry Sidley was approaching the restaurant. His jowls wobbled in time with his rapid and efficient footsteps. He arrested abruptly as he got to the door.

'Boy,' Keith said, 'Sidley sure looks irritated at the sight of Jones, the footballer and Marcus chatting away. Look, he's suddenly found something interesting on the specials board.'

Sidley looked at the 'Today's Specials' board displayed outside the restaurant. Like a plump moth with big eyes and ashen cheeks, he was drawn into the lobby area by the activity of Marcus' party. He did not wish to be detected so he fluttered in silently and settled next to the wall for cover.

Heggie clocked his wristwatch. 'Now Jones and Usavio will leave the restaurant.' Sidley fluttered to deeper cover. 'Look, Sidley is feigning an interest in the dessert trolley so he's not seen! Marcus will return to his table and collect his stuff.'

Marcus picked up a big bundle of papers from his table and casually returned to the counter to make his payment.

Keith could see that on the front of the lovely pink file containing a wedge of papers were two words, printed in big, black letters. Marcus' hand was obscuring the first word but Keith could clearly see the second which read 'DEAL'.

Sidley could see it too - and he was desperate to discover the first word.

Marcus moved around to his right.

Sidley moved round to Marcus' right from behind the dessert trolley.

Marcus swung gently back.

Sidley sidled back to his earlier position too.

Marcus made a quick and exaggerated turn and looked out through the windows of the restaurant across the plaza.

Sidley's head popped up quick behind Marcus. It turned to one side, peering at the file over Marcus' shoulder. It was like watching an idiotic chicken trying to get some grain from a covered dish, jerking, turning sideways to examine the food with one beady eye, wobbling its red, dangly chin.

Marcus patted his pockets as if he was looking for something and he moved the file flat to his chest; terminating any opportunity the chicken had left to beady-eye the writing.

Keith looked at the floor around Marcus' feet to see if he could spot what Marcus had appeared to have lost.

Sidley gave a sly look around on the floor as well.

Keith looked back at Marcus' table.

Sidley did the same.

'Marcus has left some stuff on his table, shall I get it for him?' asked Keith.

'Excuse!' hollered Heggie again in the direction of the maitre D and 'sit down,' in the direction of Keith. Keith again jumped, so much that he spat his last bit of cheesecake across the table.

'Oh, do excuse me, you made me jump again Heggie,' Keith said rather embarrassingly looking at the cheesecake projectiles on the table.

'Yes sir?'

'The bill please, we're in a frightful hurry,' said Heggie, making the internationally recognised gesture of signing ones name in the air.

'Sorry Keith, that's the last time I will make you jump in this restaurant, I just needed to divert the waiter from starting to clear Marcus' table.'

Keith could see the sly old dog Sidley, not one to stand on ceremony, had bypassed the maitre D and arrived at his usual table – table 21, the one Marcus had dined at. He was fingering through the pieces of paper Marcus had left. Sidley had no idea that Marcus had not dined with Jones and Usavio. The scene that had been presented to Sidley was quite different from reality. He looked up to see Marcus leaving the restaurant, but chose not to call after him.

'Phase one complete!' declared Heggie triumphantly. 'This is a hoot! Come on Keith, to the studio!'

At Gatwick airport, the Hat sat on a high stool at a bench outside a coffee house and watched the antics of a tattooed man. The tattooed man stood in the crowd of people waiting for the transatlantic flight from Miami to land.

The tattooed had made up a sign from a piece of cardboard he'd found in a bin outside the newsagents and wrote on it in small letters 'stop reading my sign'.

It worked a treat and kept him amused for an hour whilst he waited. Disorientated passengers came through the doors and would gravitate closer to read the writing. When they tumbled his joke, they would look up at him and he would growl at them. He was a scary and imposing figure and he enjoyed watching them scuttle off.

On the other side of the sign the Hat could see that he had written 'cellmate'. The Hat thought this was his prime suspect. The tattooed man waited until he saw his connection before turning the sign around to his own delight.

'Idiot,' the American passenger called him and punched him bang on his nose. The two exchanged a further blow each before walking out of the airport together.

The Hat knew he had found his men.

Chapter 29

Operation 'The Fat King Music Listening Studio' Phase 2
Pressing the Flesh

Heggie and Keith arrived at Trafalgar Square and made their way to the office Fuzzy Cat had located.

Keith gazed up at the facades of the offices which fronted one of the most iconic of locations in London.

'Wow, this is dead posh. We're going to have to pay thousands to rent an office facing the square for the size we need,' not seeing how this was ever going to be possible.

'This way Keith,' said Heggie leading Keith across the square to amazingly grand building. It rose from pavement level up at least five storeys as far as Keith could tell by counting the windows. The mellow yellow stone facade was impressive; big square blocks, each having been given a pitted pattern by the stonemasons who had carved them hundreds of years ago. Each storey was marked with a band of more ornately carved yellow stone. The stonemason's legacy held strong, even though with the passing of the generations the connectivity to the present day was broken. Who would know the stonemason's hand now? It was an equally magnificent and lasting creation when compared to the works that hung from the walls of the gallery across the way. There were no names to bander around of these artists. The work remained silent, unattributed. Keith thought how sad this was. He could be a sensitive fellow at times.

Heggie stepped forward and opened a rather grand looking solid oak door. It was a large, heavy wooden door with glass panels and bright polished, smooth brass furniture; smoothed by years of use and being polished on what looked like a daily basis. The door must have silently witnessed well over 200 years of hustle and bustle of the square, possibly more.

The inside of the building however was different from the majesty portrayed by the stonework and the grand old door. The hallway appeared cheap. It was large - granted, but shabby. The original space had been severed by a further set of internal doors, unpainted, roughly put together with the pencil marks to guide the carpenter still showing. The first leaves of autumn had blown into the hallway and hadn't been cleared away.

Heggie opened the door on the left hand side. It opened about a centimetre and stuck against the door surround. Heggie gave it a firm push and the structure wobbled as the door swung open. Behind the door was a very narrow corridor leading to a very narrow staircase.

'They've split the lovely old original staircase in two, that's why it's so narrow. I think they have mullered it but that's only my opinion,' said Heggie as he trudged up the stairs.

At the top, they reached another, equally poorly installed door. Heggie opened it slightly and paused. Turning to Keith he declared, 'and now for the office!'

Heggie swung the door half open and it banged against something on the other side.

The office was only about nine foot by seven foot - tops, enough for a small desk and one filing cabinet – if they were placed at an angle. The

217

scant office furniture hindered the door from being opened fully.

'Crikey, how are we going to run an operation from in here?' Keith asked. 'I suppose the view is quite something, what a lovely half a window. I like this half-a-window,' he said as he looked out onto the Square from the enormous opening which covered that entire side of the office. Even the grand old window had been butchered into two halves.

'Fuzzy Cat has a very keen spatial awareness - almost bordering on the fanatical. He spotted that this office backs onto the offices we are about to go and have a look at.'

Heggie led Keith back down the narrow stairs and around the rear of the building via a side alley. On the approach, the tall buildings each side made the alley feel even smaller and dim where they blocked out the light. The alley was quiet and Keith could hardly believe that it was just yards from one of the busiest places in London.

'I'm not sure I like it down here, it gives me the willies,' said Keith, physically shivering with the idea of being alone on a dark evening.

'We won't use this entrance; we will knock through from the office facing the square. Have a look at this.'

Heggie proceeded through another difficult-to-open doorway and up eight, wide flights of steps. This was the original aspect and it had a much pleasanter feel.

'You wouldn't think this, the eighth story was on the same level at the other office, would you? You didn't notice the downhill of the alley did you Keith it was so gradual. Only a Policeman could spot something like that!'

Heggie was now puffing hard but still patting the walls and the banister and such things, commenting on their solidness and honesty. Keith's chest had gotten tight. *'I need to do something about this – I can't even get up six flights of steps easily anymore.'* They went up two more flights of stairs, small steps they were, dead posh, three-quarter the height of normal ones they were so posh, and nicely carpeted too. Quiet, posh, stairs.

Heggie pushed the doors on the eighth floor open, revealing a black void. He went into the dark and Keith could hear him patting the wall trying to find the light switches. Heggie clicked a series of light switches which had no immediate effect. There seemed so many clicks and the illumination process was so slow that Keith began to expect a ballroom. Row upon row of lights flickered into life, running the length of a large space until they reduced into just two light sets at the end as the building narrowed towards the square.

All the windows on this level were boarded up and painted black and it all looked pretty dusty with some remnants of gym equipment and a boxing ring in the centre.

On the nearest window cill was a Tescos plastic bag. Keith's father was a Tescos bag person. A Tesco's bag was a practical, no-nonsense method of transporting things. It wouldn't have surprised Keith if he popped up next, the day was that strange.

'Probably used this for some unauthorised bouts, seen some brutal action I guess,' Keith said wandering around the void.

'You get all of this for a quarter of the price of the other office,' Heggie announced, almost triumphantly like the deal was already done.

'Have we taken a lease on this place then?'

'Nope, not yet but hopefully by the end of the day…,' Heggie paused, lowered his voice and continued, '….it will be ours…. Come on, you'll need these,' and Heggie rummaged in the plastic bag he took from the shelf and handed Keith a small plastic box with a button on it and a file containing some sheets of typed paper in a cardboard file. That figured; it was Heggie's practical, no-nonsense way of transporting things about.

'Ooh, a gadget 'eh? Looks nice.'

'That's a remote control and this is a dossier on the people who are interested in the advertising space on the side of a building newly acquired in Trafalgar Square.'

'We haven't got any of that either, have we?'

'By the end of the day Keith…. it will be ours… by the end of the day Keith.'

'I'm getting it now Heggie, I'm so getting it now. Sorry for being such a dunce.'

'We've got about 30 minutes before we meet the interested parties, so have a look through the crib sheets I've prepared and familiarise yourself with your target. I thought you could take Bernard Laitex; he's a bit of a creep but he'll be okay with you.'

Keith flicked the file open. Bernard Laitex's crib sheet was on top of the pile. Keith began to read.

Name: *Bernard Laitex.*
Company: *'Owen Cash Financial Services'.*
Position and influence in company: *Founder, holds the purse strings.*
Characteristics: *Wears his shirt undone to show his chest hair and medallion. Needs high profile recognition - all of the time, irrespective of cost. He would say that his company staff are always pleased to see him, especially the*

girls - says he brings a little something special to the office environment. They say 'you wouldn't want to get caught in a lift with those roving hands' and 'hide everyone, here he comes'.

Crowning glory: *Winning a shortlist place for four large contracts from the US – now needs to raise profile of company for the visiting US Executives.*

Worst moment: *The incident with the mop head and cleaner's uniform in the office cupboard.*

Weakness: *Mop heads and cleaners' uniforms.*

Killer Question: *'Is that disinfectant I can smell?'*

'So, I've drawn the pervert,' thought Keith. *'Wonder who else we have assembled?'* The next sheet was that of Kerry Oaki, Marcus' target.

Name: *Kerry Oaki.*

Company: *'Basse Entertainment Co'.*

Position and influence in company: *Company Director - new ventures and advertising. Brings home the bacon; highest earning executive in the company - by far.*

Characteristics: *Well respected but a bit of a good time girl. Late evenings entertaining and will spend the company cash. Has a liking for the younger man – if anyone is in her sights – they don't stand a chance! Roughly the same age as Marcus – known to each other.*

Crowning glory: *Attributed by many to have started the silent disco movement.*

Worst moment: *Being thrown out of her own silent disco at Glastonbury for trying to sing on stage after too many tequilas.*

Weakness: *Younger men, Tequila and stages – in that order.*

Killer Question: *'Was that you I saw on stage at Glasto? Did you want me to send you the footage I recorded?'*

The parade continued with Amelia's target.

Name: *William Board (Bill to his colleagues).*

Company: *'Earl E. Bird Advertising Executives'.*

Position and influence in company: *Young thruster making his way up through the company. Twice a week at least he takes the carousel taxi to spend 22 hours in the workplace. Currently being courted by Basse Entertainment Company to join them as an Exec Director - with the likelihood of being vamped by Kerry Oaki.*

Characteristics: *Young, dynamic, on the up - his star is rising.*

Crowning glory: *Securing advertising space on the US Shuttle.*

Worst moment: *Yet to come… probably with Kerry Oaki.*

Weakness: *If confined in a position with a powerful, dominant business woman, may find himself obliging.*

Killer Question: *'Would you like to join me and Kerry for dinner to give you some thinking time - or would you like to sign the paperwork now?'*

Fuzzy had two representatives from a weight loss and exercise company.

Names: *Hugh Jass and Jim Shorts.*

Company: *'Diet and Don't Die't-in the Gym'.*

Position and influence in company: Owners.

Characteristics: Go getters, super fit, super rich Australian beefcakes.

Crowning glory: Taking their company to the biggest chain of gyms in Australia with the highest number of Twitter followers - due to their banter and sound advice. Now trying to recreate that in the UK market.

Worst moment: Launching the colonic cleaner pill which effectively grounded six million Australians for a week, costing the economy $21m - and leading to their hasty relocation to the UK.

Weakness: They have no personal weaknesses, as they will tell you frequently.

Killer Question: 'Do you know where the nearest lav is; I'm on this new Australian regime of colon care?'

Heggie went for the mirror man and had picked the lunatic musician.

Name: Harry Beau Candy.

Company: 'Iona Music Studio'.

Position and influence in company: Founder, director and dictator.

Characteristics: As lively as a bucket of frogs, unpredictable in the extreme, baiter of the establishment, delusional, depressed at being out of the limelight, paranoid – it goes on...

Crowning glory: Ten top ten hits in the top ten hit parade.

Worst moment: Second album flop.

Weakness: Sweets and booze, in no particular order and mixed, usually.

223

'It's time Keith. Let's go out into the square,' Heggie called across from where he was laying in the boxing ring, staring up at the lights.

'Bernard will be standing next to the left hand lion as you look away from the building. Meet and greet him and have a chat, show him that you have done your homework. You will see from the file that you'll be safe with him and he's really the one we think will go for this – now and in the future.'

'At three o'clock - point your what's-it that you so admired at the window you so admired. The price for the space is £35,000 for a year to advertise, which, between me and you, covers the rental cost of both premises, and some. Give him this card, bid him good luck and say no more after that.'

Keith looked at the card; it simply gave Amelia's name and a mobile telephone number.

I'll meet you back over by the railings but keep walking down the same street we walked before. Marcus, Amelia and Fuzz all have their targets and I'll be around as well, just in case anything goes wrong.

'Hello, I'm Keith – you must be Bernard. How are you?'

'I'm wonderful, as my staff will tell you; particularly the ladies,' Bernard replied, singing the word 'ladies' and wobbling his fingers about. 'Plenty of totty around today, it's boot weather so I'm enjoying myself.'

Keith didn't think people like Bernard existed any more.

'Hi Kerry, good to see you again.   Can't believe I missed the silent disco thing!'

'You've had your fair share of success; time to let the younger ones have a go!   Hello Marcus darling,' she said embracing him and giggling at her own leg pulling.

Looking over Marcus' shoulder as they clinched, she said with a purr, 'there's Bill, we simply must say hello. I must have him... working for me that is.'

'Easy tiger,' said Marcus, though he really thought 'easy cougar'.

'Hi Bill, I'm Amelia. How's it going?'

'Great thank you, really looking forward to whatever it is you have planned.   Say, could we move this way a bit so I can get a better view?'

'Of course. The best view will be over here.' Amelia guided Bill towards the fountain; away from Kerry.

'Now you two chaps must be Hugh and Jim, good afternoon.'

'How ya doin' maite,' they both said together and each gave Fuzzy a firm handshake.

'Let me have look at you,' Hugh said, still holding onto Fuzzy's hand.

'He's got a good frame hasn't he Hugh,' Jim said in his broad native Australian and slapping Fuzzy on the back of the shoulder. The friendly blow made Fuzzy's hair flop over his face.

'Bit of work mate and a few supplements and he'll be just like us Jim.' They sounded identical and they both flexed their biceps at the same time towards Fuzzy.

'Work out do you – what's your name… Hell Jim, we don't even know this guy's name and we've already signed him up for one of our classes!'

Jim slapped Fuzzy on the other shoulder. 'What's your name maite?' The second friendly blow ruffled Fuzzy's suit jacket so it pulled up around his shoulders.

'I'm a member of Her Majesty's Police Force I'll have you know!' Fuzzy said haughtily but lamely. 'We are a fit, fighting force. Keeping order on the streets of this fair land, making sure our visitors to these shores are both safe and prosperous!' Fuzzy straightened his suit jacket and his hair sharply.

'Fair dinkum mate. You're apples.'

'There he is, how are you Harry my old chum?' Heggie welcomed.

'I'm fine, why - what have you heard?' Harry said furtively.

'Still top of your game I see. Looking well.'

'I'm busy you know – it's all go with the label.'

'Good to hear it.'

'And you?'

'All a bit quite really. You might like what we have got going on today.'

'Race you across the fountain? I think you are two one up in the series. Your Rome and Barcelona to my Madrid if I remember correctly.'

'Too cold and I'm too old, my dear friend.'

'Ah, you're admitting defeat then, eh?'

At three o'clock, after some more unpleasant pleasantries with Bernard, Keith pressed the button.

A banner slowly uncoiled over the large window Keith had been admiring.

Half the banner read:

'YOUR COMPANY HERE!'

and the other half, much to Keith's delight, read

'THE FAT KING MUSIC LISTENING STUDIOS – COMING SOON'.

'Wow,' thought Keith, 'free advertising and the cost of the rental on two offices in one unfurling of a banner.'

Four people clapped in the square in appreciation of the event unfolding before them.

Keith clapped too and let out a whoop, a previously suppressed, 'your next station is Great Missenden' kind of a whoop. When he was quite finished, he handed Bernard the card as instructed.

It took a while for Keith to catch up with Heggie who clearly had a spring in his step now. The rest of the gang were gravitating towards the narrow street leading to the office. Behind him, Keith could hear Amelia's telephone ringing.

'Phase two complete,' Keith thought, rubbing his hands together.

Five people, walking apart but jubilantly in the same direction, rounded the corner which led back to the larger offices.

A group of builders were unloading large glass screens from the back of a lorry. Emblazoned over them was 'Great Missenden's <u>only</u> bookmaker'.

'Fancy that Heggie, part of the hometown!' Keith said. He paused and then cringed. 'This, of course, is part of the plan and once again, I'm a few steps behind, aren't I?'

Chapter 30

Operation 'The Fat King Music Listening Studio' Phase 3
Creating Smoke and Mirrors, and More Smoke

'It's phase three Keith dear boy. Fuzzy Cat has 'borrowed' these screens from the Robinson brothers. Fuzzy made their arrest this morning and the brothers are still in custody for questioning. Fuzzy has called the screens in for forensics 'in London'. These are from their bookies – it could have easily read 'Prestwood's only bookmaker,' had you not stood your ground Keith.'

'I thought that Fuzzy had retired now?'

'Technically he has, yesterday was his last day but he is owed two days leave, so he is making very good use of his warrant card.'

Keith and Heggie followed the screens up the eight flights of stairs to the first floor. An electrician was connecting an assortment of cables to the back of a big table top bank of lights and buttons.

'This looks like a complicated bit of kit,' commented Keith, 'lots of slidey things.'

'Another of Fuzzy's acquisitions. The force has lost one very resourceful officer. Marcus tipped him off that there was an illegal party in the basement of the telephone exchange in Great Missenden, run by none other than.... you guessed it, the Robinson Brothers. So Fuzzy walked right up to the DJ booth at 5am this morning, stopped 150 people from dancing and closed it right down. Flashed his warrant card he did, right after the final set! Told everyone it was time to go home.'

'He's got courage!'

'Well, he did wait 'till the end of the night which I thought was jolly decent of him – community spirited policing! He'd been there since midnight doing, what he told me was surveillance. I can see him now, in the middle of the action, tie wrapped round his forehead, leather patches on his jacket sleeves popping all over the place, nervous twitches looking like a jerky form of dancing, right there in the centre of the dance floor.

'He announced to the 'boos' of the crowd that he had put 50 quid behind the counter at the station kiosk over the road, should, as he put it 'any of you disco dancers fancy a pot of tea, a coffee or a currant bun.' It's possibly the only time in British Policing history that a serving officer has closed down an illegal party to cheers and pats on the back from the revellers. Fuzzy tells me poor Lesley didn't know what had hit her at that time of the morning!'

Heggie's eyes glinted. He was alive. 'Alive' was the third of the three words that Keith would use to describe Heggie. He was alive with life, he was lively and he was living life. He needed to live life to be alive.

In Amersham, the Robinson brother's solicitor had just secured their release from the Police station. They were boarding the Metropolitan line train to Baker Street. It was a slow train but they were sure they would arrive just in time to witness Amelia's big deal. Who knows what would fall out of it for them - after some pressure had been applied.

There were at least 20 workmen putting large wooden panels together on a wooden stud framework in the room Heggie had shown Keith earlier.

'Come on lads,' shouted Heggie in encouragement, 'we've only got 20 minutes 'till phase four.'

This of course meant nothing to anyone else in the room, but the men seemed to pump in the nails from their air compressed guns even faster.

'Keith, could you possibly unwrap that reclining chair? These guys are doing some work on the floor above so we've popped them a large wedge for drink to build this shell, and on the promise that they get first dibs on the full refurbishment job.'

Keith unwrapped the large and plush black leather chair from its bubble wrap.

'Jump in the chair Keith, pop these on and we will see if this thing works,' said Heggie, passing Keith some plush headphones.

Keith reclined and put on the head gear which seemed to cover most of each side of his head. The headphones were comfy and the leather surrounds sat nicely over his ears, sinking a little inwards to make a snug fit.

Two of the workmen carried the screens across between Heggie and Keith and put them into position on top of a makeshift wooden dwarf wall. This completed the glass frontage of the control room and encased Heggie away from Keith. The 'Great Missenden's only bookmaker' sign obscured Heggie's face. He dimmed the lights in his booth and disappeared completely, but, just for fun he turned them up again briefly, having lined up his eyes with the 'oo' of the bookmaker. Heggie pushed and slid a number of buttons and his voice came through the headphones.

'I know this is one of your favourites Keith, lay back and enjoy.' Heggie's voice faded out and Barry Manilow's 'One Voice' filled Keith's ears, and due to the isolation, had the sensation of filling his whole head.

Keith had a giggle and gazed up into the darkness and then closed his eyes. The music seemed to be a lot closer and more defined. He could only just hear the bustle of the workmen and the odd thud as another nail went into the wooden construction. *'This place has a very good feel about it,'* he thought. The track ended and the music faded away. Heggie's voice came back through the earphones.

'Okay Keith, you've got to make yourself scarce, we're expecting someone who may recognise you. Pop through that door on your left and you can watch proceedings from there. I'm sure you'll find a suitable crack between one of the panels.'

Heggie's mobile phone illuminated the gloom and the ringtone purred like a cat. 'Fuzzy Cat Mobile' showed on the display.

'Hi D-I,' Heggie said into the phone and turned to Keith and mouthed 'Ho-de-ho' with a giggle and a wriggle of his shoulders.

The studio was dead silent and Keith could hear Fuzzy speaking.

'Do you know someone called Frank Roberts?' Fuzzy asked.

'Now there's a name from the past; he was married to my mum for a while – nasty piece of work. Why do you ask?'

'Cheese says he's just arrived in Gatwick. I've spoken to the intelligence services - they don't know why he's come to England but he's just met up with a guy wanted for stealing two cars in Prestwood and Great Missenden – the Robinson brother's cars, so he can't be all that bad. They're unsure if the car thief knows the Robinsons but they've linked both of the men to you. What's this all about Heggie?'

'He's probably come across to get me back for that lengthy prison sentence he served for trying to kill me. It should be okay though, they won't know I'm here in London and hopefully the Police will pick them up soon.'

'They're sending a police car to your house as I'm sure they will be heading there.'

'Why didn't the police pick Roberts up at the airport?'

'Spent sentences – nothing to account for. They had put the stolen car under surveillance at the airport hoping to pick up the thief; but he's gone and stolen another car from the airport car park so the Police have lost their whereabouts. The Police have rated him 4 out of 5 on the chainsaw scale – he's a dangerous man!'

'Holey smoley, this is all we need today! What does the other guy look like?'

'Mean looking American fella, about 65, well built, broad and about six foot six inches. Would stand out in any crowd but his distinguishing features are lots of tattoos, particularly the visible stars on his neck and half an ear he lost to Roberts in a cell fight.'

Keith heard all of the conversation. There couldn't have been two American men in England matching that description. Keith had led him directly to the village where Heggie was living. He felt sick in the pit of his stomach.

Heggie clicked off his phone.

'I'm sorry Heggie, that sounds like the bloke I gave directions to that time in London, the one looking for rock legends. It appears that I led him right to our village.'

233

'Don't worry about it, they would have found me anyway if they wanted. It's something I've been waiting for, so it will be good to get it over and done with. The girls are away from the house anyway so they're safe, but it would account for the strange goings on, wouldn't it?'

Keith stepped out from the inner part of the makeshift studio where the chair sat, through the chipboard door, hung with some fairly basic and clumsy hinges. From the outside, the shell looked so small and peculiar sat within the void of the rest of the building space. It wobbled and shook as Keith closed the door behind him.

Heggie's mobile phone illuminated and purred again. Heggie answered and put it onto speaker so Keith could hear.

'There's some further bad news. The Robinson brothers are out and are heading this way. The British Transport Police are monitoring them; and they've reached Baker Street. If they're coming here – and I know they don't usually go outside their patch, only when I invite them to Amersham nick, their ETA will be about 25 minutes.'

Heggie said nothing in response but thanked the DI for the news.

'They don't know where we are Keith, don't worry – I know you so enjoyed meeting them before!'

Keith could see Heggie doing his final checks, setting the levels and testing all of the buttons.

There was a flash at the end of Heggie's fingertips and then there was pitch darkness. There was a period of silence.

'Heggie – are you okay?'

'Crikey Charlie, this isn't part of the plan Keith in case you were wondering, but yep, I'm okay. These things come in threes they say.'

Amelia burst through the door.

'He's here.   He's with Marcus downstairs.
What on earth is going on in here?   I can smell
burning.'

Chapter 31

Operation 'The Fat King Music Listening Studio' Phase 4
Doing the Deal and Dealing with the Americans

'It's only my hair,' Heggie shouted. 'Amelia, get the electrician back down here and make sure Marcus keeps our target talking.' As Amelia turned to exit, Heggie called after her, 'Amelia, we may get some un-invited guests, unlikely but a possibility - they're not for you to deal with – stay well away from them. Get me if they appear.'

'Okay, but who are they?'

'You won't know them. Two of them are from America – both nasty. One looks like a ferret and the other one is huge and has tattoos and half an ear missing.'

'Oh, just like the man I saw in the bookmakers in Great Missenden......'

Well the other two you may just know then, they're the Robinson Brothers, they own that bookies – they own the screens and the sound equipment we're using. It's okay though, they won't have a clue where we are in London.'

'Oh dear.... they might do.... I may have blabbed when I was trying to get a dinner date. You know me and dangerous men, sorry!' she said in a wince.

'The tattooed man wouldn't have overheard you by any chance?'

Amelia winced further. Heggie knew it was a possibility.

'Well, your luck's in – you're going to be surrounded by dangerous men before the hour is out.'

The electrician arrived quite rapidly. Heggie shouted something in what Keith thought was a European tongue. From somewhere near the electrician's torch beam that was strapped to his head, the reply came back. Heggie interpreted. 'It's just as he thought, the fuse had blown on this level.'

'How long?' Heggie shouted to the electrician, his voice was frantic.

'Twenty five.'

'Too long, we need power now. Is there another source?'

'I suppose I could run a cable down from the second floor.'

'How long?' asked Heggie again.

'Fifteen minutes, but you can't rush these things.'

'Can you rig something else up that would take less time?'

'You still need some sort of power source.' There was silence. The beam of the electrician's torch started moving around the void. It moved up and down like a robotic fairground waltzer, randomly shining on various objects. It stopped and illuminated the redundant sports equipment and flitted between the various objects. The torch moved and rose up and then there was a whirl of pedals.

'We could rig up this exercise bike – that might give us enough power,' the electrician's voice said.

'Okay, let's start with that whilst we try and sort a more permanent fix out.'

'You'll need to keep it running – and only five minutes,' the electrician said, second guessing Heggie's next question.

'I'll take it! Fuzzy, Fuzzy, where are you?' Heggie called out. Keith saw a movement in the gloom now that his eyes had become accustomed to the darkness. Fuzzy stepped forward making Keith jump.

'You're like a panther in the night. Hi, I'm Keith.'

'Your shed changed my life....'

'Go,' shouted the electrician, having connected a cable to the resistor on the front wheel.

'Pumpo,' shouted Heggie. Fuzzy sprang up onto the saddle and began to pedal like a good 'un. His hair was flopping about side to side and his moustache appeared to stand directly outwards, parallel with the bottom of his nose. Fuzzy's brown suit trousers were flapping with the speed of his rotations and his chicken wing twitch had gone into overdrive. Keith had never seen a man more committed to a cause, almost as if his whole future depended on it.

The buttons on the desk glowed a little and as Fuzzy peddled up, more of the bank of lights flickered into being.

'You can only run the music system and this desk light off the bike,' the electrician explained.

A great shaft of light filled the room as the door was pushed wide open. Keith saw Sidley-Smith come marching in ahead of Marcus and Amelia. He stood a few foot in, pulled up his suit jacket around his waist and put his hands firmly on his hips. He surveyed the area.

'Yes, yes,' he said, his head twitching all over the place like a plucky hen with a beady eye for some freshly thrown corn.

'This is the first booth – it's an individual listening booth,' Marcus said, 'we're building twenty of the individual listening booths.'

'Yes, yes,' said Sidley, demandingly ushering them in further.

'We're also having twenty group listening areas, a live set up area linked to a social enclosure so bands can try out their new tracks on guests, dark areas, chill out areas, water tanks and the latest in sensory experience, the intravenous music lab.'

'Not heard of the intravenous experience before,' clucked Sidley.

'Not been invented yet,' replied Marcus, 'I've been working on it for 15 years now. You, Mr Sidley-Smith, are the only person in whole world outside my research and development team, 'Pump, Armstrong and Emperors', to have heard about it.'

Sidley visibly bristled with pleasure.

'A world first 'eh!' he boomed, teasing the end of his moustache. 'That'll turn a few heads in the village that will,' he said a bit more quietly. Sidley tugged the end of his moustache. 'There he goes,' they'll say as I glide onto the platform, 'he did it first you know, first in the world!' Sidley was thinking; goodness knew where he had gone to in his head. 'Mmm,' Sidley said louder and declared to the room, 'I can do first in the world.'

'I'm afraid we can't let you see the other booths,' Marcus said, bringing Sidley back from global domination with intravenous music, 'glitch with the insurance. Go on, jump on into the seat and get yourself comfortable.'

'Don't mind if I do,' Sidley said returning to his deep authoritarian voice and once again commandeering the situation. He whipped off his jacket and threw it over to Marcus without looking. Sidley had the most outrageously thick braces holding up his trousers and before he sat down, he adjusted them by running this thumbs from his shoulders down to his waistband and back up again. Sidley relaxed back into the chair. *'One Voice,'* thought Keith.

After about two and a half minutes of pure silence in the room, Sidley shouted out a loud, staccato 'more!' The track played through, denoted by the silence and the cry 'more' from the chair went up a further two times.

'That will be Cococabana and the Bermuda Triangle then,' Keith whispered to Fuzzy. Fuzzy nodded and a bead of sweat rolled from his nose.

'Move on – not that one!' Sidley shouted.

'He obviously didn't like that track then! He's a victim of not understanding how loud he is speaking!' chucked Keith in Fuzzy's direction. Fuzzy's head had dropped a bit, as had his rotation rate. Sweat was now running from his scalp, making his thin hair appear even thinner.

Given the quietness, only edged by the soft whirl of Fuzzy's wheels, everyone in the room, apart from Sidley that was, could hear the unmistakable grinding and squeaking sound of the downstairs door opening. It was unlikely to be the workmen – they used the side door and back staircase as an entrance to the floors above. If time could race, it was racing at this moment – speeded on by collective minds processing the reality that their unwanted guests had arrived.

Heggie jumped up from the desk of electronics.

'Marcus, you need to take over – I need to sort these visitors out.'

Heggie walked across to the door. A momentary shaft of light appeared and was then gone, leaving behind it a sickly worried atmosphere.

Heggie crossed the hallway and started to go down the stairs, his heart was pounding so much it seemed to be in his throat. He tried to gulp it back down and be cool.

Down one flight of stairs he went. Nothing. Not a sound.

Down the second flight of stairs. Nothing either. He padded on quietly and gingerly, downwards. He stopped and looked down the central space between the last two flights of stairs. He cocked his head to one side, straining to listen for the slightest sound. The hallway and stairs were carpeted. It helped him move silently; but didn't help him detect the movement of anyone else though.

He started down the first of the last two flights. Slowly, carefully. The only sound he could hear was his pulse, throbbing in his ears. His adrenaline was pumping. He was shaky and he felt he could crumple at any moment, his stomach and hips were that weak with fear. He knew the danger had to be within the next 30 or so steps.

'I could call out and engage them,' he thought. That might take some of the suspense away. He elected to keep quiet and carried on creeping painfully slowly down the stairs.

He stood on the last landing before the bottom. His brain was white with terror. He knew it was going to be an awful encounter and he may end up properly injured if things were as serious as they might be. He wasn't sure just how mad his step father would be – but he guessed it was pretty serious, given the trip to England. He knew he wasn't about to get just the 'I'm really disappointed in you step son' talk. He could see the door now, slightly ajar, stuck on the floor where it had been opened. The door was problematic and it hung about three millimetres to low – scraping on the floor at about three inches into the opened position.

Had the wind just blown it open? Was he being silly and over alert? What would Robert's do anyway? Surely he would only want to give him a rough up; tell him what he thought of him and how he had thought about nothing else whilst he was inside.

Fifteen steps left. He took two of them. The ground floor was split between the stairs and a corridor which went along and back under the stairs to provide a storage area. It was spacious; with the broad stairs and hallway being at least eight foot wide in this old building.

'Tough men don't hide under stairs. They face you up – come straight for you; not hide away.' He took another two steps down and peered carefully over the banister to try and see if he could see anyone in the storage area. Nothing, just gloom and no movement.

'But why had Roberts come all this way?' Heggie's mind raced, searching for some sort of comfort. The comfort wasn't forthcoming. He kept thinking that it sure as hell wasn't to say 'hello' and it was all a 'terrible misunderstanding' and how about 'being friends'.

The draught caused by the slightly ajar door puffed across Heggie's face. The slight movement of the wind was enough to make him freeze. *'He's come to finish the job!'* he thought. *'He wouldn't mind going back inside for this; that's just his nature. Do the time – for an actual crime, this time.'*

Heggie was creeping down close to the wall for the next five steps. This afforded him vision and time if anyone emerged from under the stairs.

As he took more steps forwards and downwards, Heggie knew it increased the risk of an encounter. Statistically he also knew that it reduced the chance of an encounter but he could only think of the former. *'It's going to happen in the next 30 seconds.'*

Heggie moved again to the banister and peered over, backwards towards the space under the stairs. Still no sound. Still no movement.

'This is ridiculous, there's no-one here. Go and open the door fully and get some light in here – provide yourself with an escape if necessary.'

Heggie boldly but quickly strode across the hallway and yanked the door. It opened quickly after un-sticking from its island on the floor and sunshine poured into the space. He turned and looked back.

'False alarm'. He looked outside. All was normal. People were going about their business and wandering around in the sunshine. Heggie stood in the sunshine for a minute. He was contented that the deal was going on upstairs and no one had shown. A family of tourists peered into a map, it was reassuring to see. *'Why d'ya get yourself so worked up Heggie. There's no problem here!'* He let the sun shine into his face and onto the back of his eyes. He had to get back to the deal.

Heggie went back through the door. Still cool, gloomy and silent - more gloomy now that he had come from the brightness - but with no danger. He pushed the door up, turned and started his run up to climb the stairs.

Roberts grabbed him with both hands around his neck and pushed him back across the hall and up against the door. Heggie was jolted to the core given his forward momentum had been savagely arrested by the oncoming Roberts.

'I've been waiting a long time for this boy,' he snarled.

Heggie's mind flashed white, whiter than on the way down the stairs.

'You're bit old for this now aren't you Frank?' Heggie responded and tried to push him away. Heggie figured that he'd be able to manhandle Frank easily. Frank must have been at least 75 years old. Frank's wiry arms stuck fast and he didn't move much, despite Heggie's best attempts. Heggie managed to move about six inches off the door.

'I shoulda taught you more of a lesson the first time!'

'Aaaagh,' screeched Amelia as she ran down the last of the stairs at full flight and jumped on Frank's back; knocking them both back into the door with the full force of an irate record executive.

Heggie's head thumped against the solid wood of the door.

Amelia now had her arms around Frank's neck, tugging him backwards and wrestling him from side to side. Her impact too was limited.

'I just can't leave you to do anything, can I?' The tattooed man emerged from the shadows and plucked Amelia from the back of Frank with one hand. His long and large arms adequately confined the ball of energy and he dragged Amelia over to the stairs and sat with her on his lap.

'I've heard you English girls like to put up a fight!' he went on, struggling her arms down and kissing her around her ear as she sat, snared between his enormous legs and arms. 'On with the show, Frank,' he encouraged.

Frank regained control of the dazed Heggie and now had him up against the wall on the other side of the hallway. There was about 15 feet between the two couples.

Frank pushed his forearm up under Heggie's throat and dropped his other arm and fumbled inside his own jacket. Frank couldn't find what he was looking for and he started to look around the floor. Heggie was pinned up, helpless, but also scanned the floor for what Frank was looking for.

The knife had been dislodged by Amelia.

Heggie's mind squirmed with the helplessness of his predicament. It was good that the knife was five foot away but Heggie knew that this was only going to delay things, not change the outcome.

Light streamed into the hallway, so bright that only the silhouettes of the entrants could be seen.

'Please be the Police,' Heggie pleaded in his own mind.

There was a pause in proceedings whilst everyone's eyes adjusted. Frank didn't go for the knife. It was only common assault at this stage – the knife could be anyone's.

'You again, troublesome,' Robinson brother number one said to Heggie, picking up the knife. 'You always seem to be getting in our way. You have some of our stuff.'

'Double bubble,' thought Heggie, not seeing how he was ever likely to get out of this one.

'You look like you need some assistance,' Robinson brother number two half enquired to Heggie and half threatened the pensioner who had him pinned up against the wall.

'What's he to you?' Frank snarled. 'He's mine – you go get your stuff; like two good boys. You're young enough for me to spank both of you – just like ya mamma used to.'

The reference to the Robinson brothers' age was bad enough – it pushed up the dial on the 'irked scale'. The reference to their mother spanking them pushed the dial into and beyond the red zone. Their mother had never spanked them, despite their difficult childhood.

The Robinson brothers turned to each other and one said, 'you would have thought this American would know that English boys love and respect their mothers.' Both of them shook their heads. He continued, 'the chap you're holding up there with those bony little arms of yours did us a huge favour once. I think we should repay him for that, don't you think brother?'

'And for 5% of whatever you have going down today – looks like you need to be looked after,' the other brother chipped in.

They waited for Heggie's nod and then one of the Robinson brothers waded in.

'That's for the ham baguettes!' the other one commentated as the fighting Robinson brother landed a blow to Frank. 'That's for the use of the shed and the dib-dabs!' as he knocked him to the floor. 'And that's for not turning us in to the Police as kids!' as the Robinson brother kicked the yank up the backside.

'Debt settled,' the fighting Robinson said as he stood over the defeated Frank, 'although we will be always grateful; we need to draw the line now.'

'Recognise the old boy sat down over there?' Robinson brother number two said to his sibling. 'Every time he pops up, we seem to lose a car.'

Robinson brother number two turned to the tattooed man. 'You don't take from the Robinson Brothers.'

'Er, hello?' Amelia said, 'what about me?'

'Hello again gorgeous.'

The tattooed man stood to his full height. He was even more impressive when he was two steps up. Amelia's feet dangled about three feet above the ground and the tattooed man kissed her again on her ear. She wrestled to get free and Robinson brother one growled his dissatisfaction. The tattooed man released Amelia and prepared to do battle.

246

Amelia ran and stood behind her dangerous hero. 'You're in for it now yankee boy!' she taunted.

'No, I think it is these Yankee boys who are in for it!' he replied calmly and he strode forward.

The battle didn't take long. One well built but aging man against two fit and young hoodlums wasn't, in the end, an equal battle. The Police arrived and carted the four of them off. Heggie and Amelia made their way back upstairs and locked the doors behind them.

After a good half hour and a few 'Bloody Nora's' from Fuzzy, Sidley raised his hand.

'Excellent he declared, enjoyed that!' He whipped out of the chair, adjusted his braces again with his thumbs and his jacket was back on as quickly as he had taken it off. 'Had a lot of interest?' he enquired.

Marcus responded. 'You're our first. In fact, we weren't expecting you! Your information must be very good.' Sidley-Smith let out a rolling grumble which started with embarrassment and ran into pride of recognition. Marcus paused for a couple of seconds to allow Sidley to revel in his triumph and then went on, 'we have a Mr Jones coming along in 20 minutes.'

'No, no. Well tell him you have all the finance you need,' boomed Sidley. '£150,000 you said with repayment after 5 years at 1.5%, share option of 15% discounted 2.5%. Oh, and one more requirement as a major investor, I would like you to name the inverted music what's-it booth after me – I do intend to come in you know!'

'We'll name it the inverted Sidley-Smith suite.'

Sidley fingered his braces again, peered into the gloom which surrounding him, pecked his head up, down and to each side and bristled at the title of the suite.

'Yes,' he declared, 'my word is my bond but you'll have a contract by the end of the day. Ha-ha, put this Jones fellow off at once.' And then to himself, but a little too loud he said, 'come along Victor victorious, carry on carring on what you do best – winning.'

Marcus and Sidley shook hands and out through the door they went.

'Got it,' the electrician announced and the lights flicked on to expose the rather pathetic and shabbily constructed shell which hadn't looked too bad at all in the darkness. Fuzzy stopped pedalling. In fact, everyone had forgotten about him and he now slid sideways like a stiff board onto one of the exercise mats and there he laid rasping for breath.

Although he should have known better by now, Keith was pondering the Jones situation. 'It's a shame we'll have to put Jones off. We could have got a better deal.'

'Keith, dear boy,' Heggie said putting his hand onto Keith's shoulder, 'there is no meeting with Jones, there never was...'

'Inspired' Keith said.

Chapter 32

Operation 'The Fat King Music Listening Studio' Phase 5
Into Operations

'Come on, phase five,' Heggie shouted, whipping his hand around in the air like he was twisting a lasso, 'drinks and job titles, this way to the bar,' throwing the imaginary lasso towards the door and pulling himself along the imaginary rope.

He looked back at Keith and said, 'you've yet to meet your business partners have you? You've been a sleeping-in-a-coma partner, up to now!'

Pop, pop. 'Champage for everybody,' Heggie cried. The champagne flowed.

'Fuzzy becomes head of security operations,' he continued.

'I'm pleased,' Fuzzy replied with a schoolboy chuckle.

'Amelia; the head of marketing and communications and any other troubleshooting we might need.'

She made an imaginary pistol shooting action which only marketing types generally tend to do these days.

'I'll set the musical directions and train the hosts to look after the guests, and after that, I'll be front of house, doing what any self respecting magazma man does best.'

'Marcus, finance, special events and growth.'

Marcus nodded and raised his glass.

'Keith,' Heggie said, 'you're the Executive Director of Operations…. that's the governor Keith to you. You're in charge. You gave us the idea, you saved me and gave us all renewed direction.'

Keith was surprised.

'And one late addition to the party with a 5% stake, in charge of muscle and urban industry watching, much, I'm sure to Amelia's delight, the Robinson Brothers.'

Everyone gasped, apart from Amelia that was, who squeaked somewhat in delight.

'No need for gasps people, I've known these kids since they were this high,' Heggie said, flattening his hand to around his knee area.

Chapter 33

Operation 'The Fat King Music Listening Studio' Phase 6
Decadence Revisited

The opening event was well attended and after the glitterati and excessive music types had gone, Keith settled into a chair in one of the booths. Heggie came through the earphones....

'This has been fun Keith hasn't it?'

Keith popped his thumb up in the direction of the darkened galley.

'We should write about this stuff. Our journey, our feelings, our caper. I know someone who I share a boundary with who can and should write. Perhaps I should talk it over with him in the shed. I think it would be fun.'

Keith pressed his lips up, turned the sides of his mouth down and bobbled his head around in that kind of 'sounds like a good idea' motion.

'Keith. We now have everything, doing what we want with new direction and meaning, perhaps more capers in the pipeline, as well as families who love us, man. Love us unconditionally for who we are. Should we be putting in check the excessive?'

Keith and Keith's mind voted yes. But I'll leave you to draw your own conclusions from the evidence before you as to whether they arrested the decadence.

The End

Post note

The Fat King Music listening studios is now in 47 locations worldwide. Copy companies have sprung up, but the Fat King remains the original and the best, overseen by the passionate and talented team who are driven by music and the desire to have fun. Okay, they diversified to meet the mass market; but you have got to have an income stream.

As for the book....., well Heggie spoke to that aspiring author he mentioned. He was thrilled and agreed to get working on it straight away, on one condition: that he used an alias – Sewel T. Whynot.